CAUSEY PIKE FROM DERWENTWATER, THE LAKE DISTRICT : J CAMPBELL KERR

WHERE'S THAT?

The approximate locations of our picture features

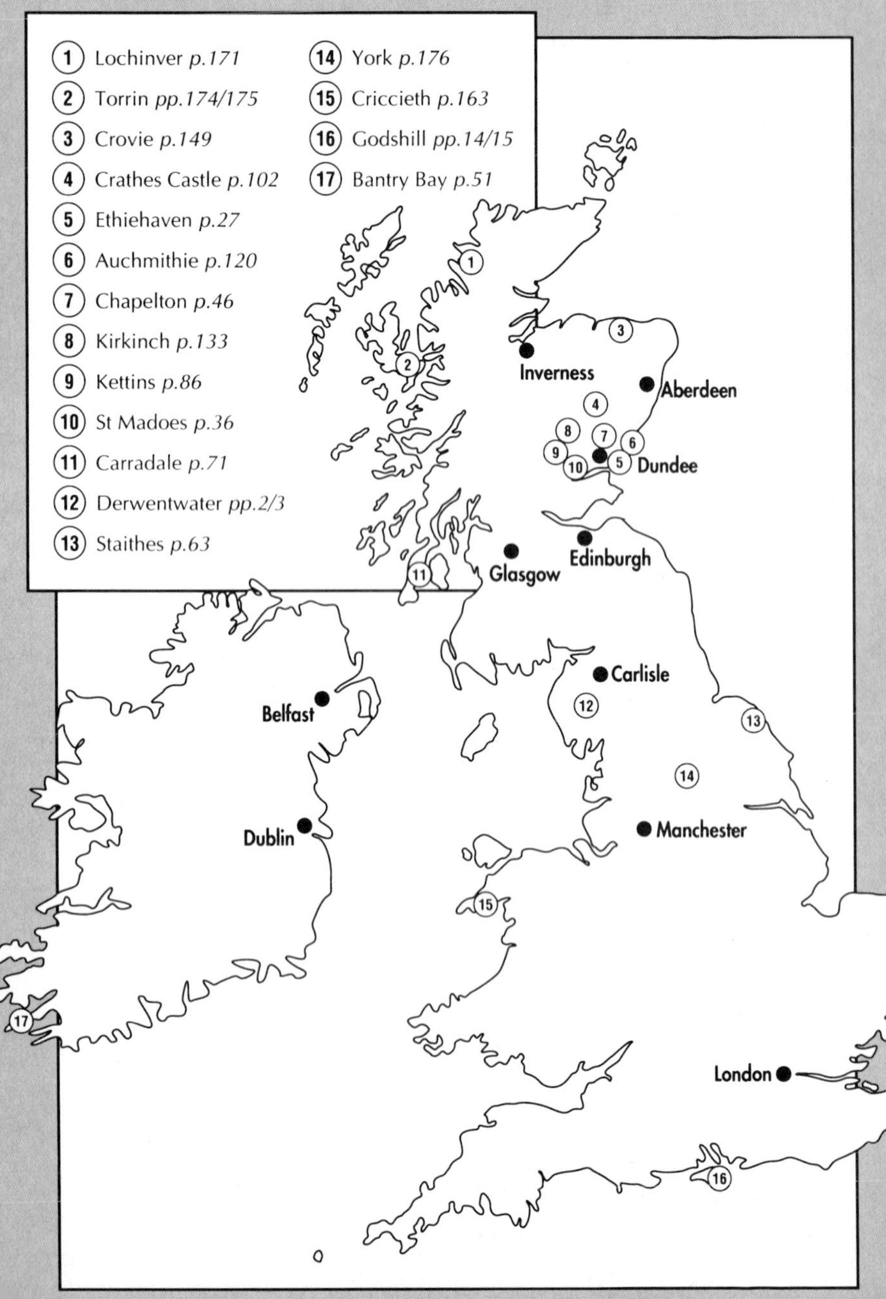

People's Friend Annual 1996

Contents

BACK COVER *York Minster from the city walls.*

At The Heart Of The Family

by OLWEN RICHARDS

SARA let the magazine she was holding fall into her lap, unread. The sun was far too strong and she would have to wait till Jenny brought her sunglasses.

Stupid of her to forget them, but then Bryony had been so difficult at breakfast, with endless questioning about her father joining them, that several things had simply slipped her mind.

Sara sighed, attempting to relax. It was impossible. The deckchair wasn't comfortable and neither were her thoughts. This holiday was the epitome of everything that had gone wrong these last few months.

She sighed again and glanced across to where the children were. Safe enough, she thought, just playing games of catch with Bryony's new beach-ball. Then she closed her eyes and let herself drift idly back a year ...

With Robert stuck in such a low-paid office job, there'd been no money that July to spare for holidays away. Still, as he pointed out, there were a lot worse off than him, without a job at all. Besides, they could have almost as much fun at home. They'd never taken Bryony round half the sights of their own town.

And so they did. It had been such a glorious week, the three of them with little cash but fewer cares. They enjoyed one another's company, taking full advantage of the places that had no admission charges, taking picnics with them or, for a special treat, searching out a cheap café.

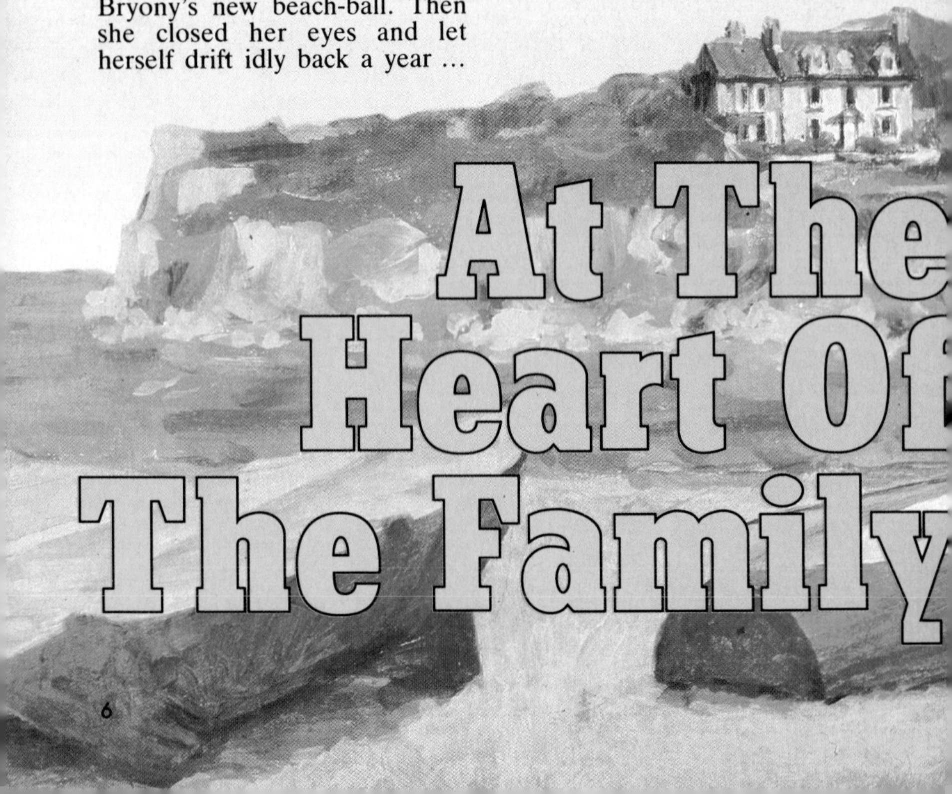

THEN August came and with it the offer of a decent job at last. The local bank. Security, a better salary and, what was more, a very real prospect of promotion if Robert proved himself.

There was a lot of studying to do, exams to pass, but nothing that he couldn't handle if he was prepared to sacrifice some of his leisure time. He was, of course. Thee wasn't anything he wouldn't do to make a good life for his family.

But the studying had gnawed relentlessly into Robert's evenings. Whereas before he'd played with Bryony and helped to get her ready for her bath and bed, now he was in the tiny spare room, bent in such deep concentration over piles of books that, when Sara dared look in at seven to disturb him, a fleeting frown would cross his face.

She'd never known him quite like this, put out by the suggestion that he kiss his little girl goodnight, and she hated it. He looked so tired, too.

"You need a holiday," she'd said the day that Bryony broke up from school.

"Nonsense," he'd replied. "I'm fine. And anyway, I couldn't simply drop my studying and swan off somewhere now. I've got exams, remember?"

How could she forget?

"Not till September, Rob. A week off in the summer wouldn't hurt. In fact, I reckon it would do us both the world of good. And Bryony."

"That's all you know about it," Rob had answered crossly.

"What *I* know is that you rarely see your daughter. You owe it to her to take time off."

"I owe it to her to get promoted, earn a better salary and take her somewhere really nice next year."

"Next year there'll be more exams and more excuses! And all the while she's growing up so fast . . . You'll never have these years with her again. We've managed to save up a bit — we can afford it, if we go self-catering . . ."

"That wouldn't be a holiday for you, to take the chores along. Without me, you could have a few days in a smart hotel."

"I'd be miserable without you. And Bryony's still too much of a tomboy for smart hotels."

"Well, find a suitable boarding-house."

Sara sighed and passed a weary hand across her forehead.

"I think you've missed the point. We *need* to be together. As a family."

"We're that all year at home," Robert said tetchily. "You simply want a break and all I'm saying is it's fine by me. Just count me out."

"I might well do that," Sara found herself retorting as the tears threatened. "I'm going to check on Bryony," she added, anxious to be out of Robert's sight before they fell. She wasn't going to show that she was hurt. Nor was she going to beg for his companionship. She'd too much pride for that.

THE guest-house wasn't smart at all. It was a vast, Victorian house whose weather-beaten front had clearly seen much better days. But inside it was clean and comfortable and the welcome was extremely warm.

"I'll show you to your room," said Mrs Cox, who wasn't much more than Sara's age herself.

"And this," she added, smiling down at Bryony, "this is your daughter? I'm sure she won't want to unpack. It's pretty boring, isn't it? Perhaps she'd like to go and play with Jamie in the garden at the back. They must be about the same age . . ."

Bryony was leaping with delight, so Sara nodded.

"They will be safe?" she murmured.

"It's all walled in. And anyway, I'll watch them through the kitchen window as I start the dinner vegetables. Which reminds me. I know you didn't book half-board, but if you'd ever like an evening meal, you only have to say. I always seem to make too much!"

"I'm pretty tired from the drive, I must admit. The thought of trailing out tonight in search of food . . ."

"Well, don't! I've got a lovely piece of beef in roasting."

"That sounds tempting!" Sara smiled.

It smelt tempting, too, the savoury aroma drifting through the hallway as they made their way upstairs.

The room was bright with flowers, the beds were crisp with freshly-laundered sheets, the basin shone. There was a television and a tray for making tea or coffee. All that she could wish for, all that would make it home from home, all except for Robert . . .

Sara was surprised to see that there were just four of them for supper.

"This is the quietest week of all," Jenny Cox said. "Term ended yesterday, so people take the weekend to get organised. You wait till Monday. We'll be bursting at the seams."

"But your husband — ?" Sara began.

"I run the business single-handed. It keeps me out of mischief," Jenny said somewhat wryly. "Peter is away at sea."

"Robert might as well be," Sara murmured, "for all we see of him."

Then, noticing the wave of loneliness that crossed the other woman's face, she felt ashamed. "I'm sorry — I didn't think. It was a silly thing to say. I didn't mean . . ."

"Don't worry. I really should be used to it by now. But," Jenny added gently, "you've got domestic problems of your own?"

It wasn't easy to explain that a well-intentioned plan to talk her husband into taking a holiday had somehow ended in a silly argument. That she'd not spoken to him in the morning, but, waiting till he'd gone to work, she'd asked around the neighbours and received a glowing testimony to the Coxes' hospitality.

"I rang at once. You said you had a vacancy and so I packed and came. I *did* leave Robert the address," Sara finished lamely, feeling suddenly ashamed of what she'd done.

"But no apology?"

"I should have, I suppose, but I was angry. And it wasn't all my fault, that row. Still, storming out was maybe going just too far. That's typical of me to act in haste and then repent at leisure."

"You could still ring him now."

"I'd not know what to say."

"Well, sleep on it tonight. You may feel better by tomorrow."

Sara tried, but sleep evaded her, and she appeared at breakfast pale and drawn, and still undecided.

"Look, this is my last day off for ages. Why don't we spend the morning on the beach?" Jenny suggested. "Bryony and Jamie could tire themselves out playing, while you and I conserve the little energy we've got left just soaking up the sun. I'll make up some sandwiches."

"That sounds terrific." Sara sighed. "And maybe later I'll get round to ringing Robert."

SO here she was, attempting to get comfortable in her deckchair while Jenny drove back to the house to fetch the bucket Jamie had forgotten and the sunglasses.

Here she was, wondering what on earth she'd say to Robert when she finally got around to phoning.

Stirring from her contemplation for a moment, Sara checked the

The Farmer And His Wife

"I'LL be glad when it's past."

I was about ten when I first heard those words, and they've stayed with me ever since.

How could Grannie, my dear Grannie, wish Christmas was past?

When you are ten years old, it seems a very long time between one Christmas and another. These few days were to be looked forward to, no matter what adults thought.

I can understand now why Gran liked to get Christmas over. We all converged on her for a Christmas Eve supper — now it would be called dinner. To my humble mind, dinner is still the meal in the middle of the day.

How she put on such a spread, I'll never know. All she had at her disposal was an open fire with an oven on one side and boiler on the other, plus a hanging spit.

I'm sorry to say Anne and I have got round to Grannie's way of thinking. We are glad when Christmas is past, but not for the same reason.

Anne won't have the grandchildren plus parents on Christmas Day for a meal. Their place is at home round their own table.

On the evening of Boxing Day she puts on a spread. It has to be in the evening, as Boxing Day is usually a shooting day when rabbits and other game are dealt with.

By night everyone is looking forward to Grannie's table weighed down with another Christmas dinner.

It's easier now for Anne than in Grannie's day. Most of the meal can be prepared in advance and put in the freezer or fridge.

Anne looks forward to all the family coming and everyone sitting round her table for that meal. To be honest, it's one of the highlights of

children were all right. Bryony's red ball was flying back and forth across an upturned dinghy. But it was far too bright for eyes that hadn't slept, she mused, and closed her heavy lids against the sun a second time . . .

Then, suddenly, there was a piercing scream. It ripped across the morning like a knife and Sara's stomach lurched. In seconds she was over by the boat and kneeling down to comfort Bryony. Carefully, she prised away the clutching hands and saw the gaping wound . . .

She was endeavouring to bind a towel round the gash and stem the blood, when Jenny reached her side.

"Thank goodness!" Sara breathed. "It's looking bad."

"The car's not far. We'll get her to the cottage hospital in minutes. Ah!" she added, as she reached for Jamie's hand. "That's what did the damage, see? A piece of broken bottle."

★ ★ ★ ★

"It's not too deep," the doctor comforted, "but maybe just a stitch or two for safety's sake . . ."

Bryony was shaking with a rhythmic sobbing now and Sara held her close.

"It's all right, sweetheart. There's nothing to be scared of. Just a pin-prick and it'll all be over."

by
John
Taylor

the year. So that isn't the reason she is glad to see Christmas past.

ANNE'S a great worrier, not for herself but for her family.

"Gran, what would you like for Christmas?" our grandchildren all ask her.

"Nothing, just come on Boxing Day. That's all I want."

That's most unhelpful as they wouldn't dream of coming without giving dear Gran a present.

When you are our age, what do you want? Only good health, and that can't be given.

The family worries and she worries about them over this present business.

I'm no problem — a book, shaving soap, or two ounces of tobacco plus matches.

Gran is the grandchildren's real headache. In the past she has received plants, a year's subscription to a ladies' magazine, and one of the boys gave her eight beautiful wee bottles of spices.

But it gets harder every year. That's why Anne wishes Christmas was past and they wouldn't feel obliged to spend the little money they have on her.

She asks the youngsters in turn what they want, but gets the answer, "I'll leave it to you."

Their respective mums sometimes ask Grannie to buy them a new jacket, a pair of jeans — if that's what you call those blue trousers — or some other piece of clothing.

Anne does as she's told but somehow she doesn't think that's a real Christmas present.

It's this annual problem which worries her, and after the Boxing Day dinner she says, "I'm pleased it's past."

The next day Grannie sits down and writes them each a letter thanking them.

There's not another Gran like her, according to our grandchildren. Long may Gran be blessed to receive their presents.

"Your daughter's had a bit of a fright," the doctor continued. "I think I'd like to keep her in a while to rest. Not long," he added, seeing Sara's worried look. "She'll be discharged tonight, most probably."

"I'd better tell my friend," Sara said. "She'll want to take her own child home."

The doctor nodded.

"You're sure you'll be OK?" Jenny asked anxiously. "There's nothing I can do?"

"We're fine. We couldn't be in better hands."

"All right." Jenny squeezed her arm. "When they let you go, just give me a ring and I'll pick you up."

Sara stood forlornly, watching Jenny disappear through the double doors. She'd meant to ask her to ring Robert, but somehow she couldn't do it.

Holding Bryony against her, Sara cursed her stupid pride. It had prompted her to come away alone instead of pleading wth her husband. Now it was preventing her from asking him to come to them in time of trouble.

It wasn't fair on Bryony, her conscience said. It wasn't fair on Robert, either, for he had a right to know. The moment that the wound was stitched, she'd ring . . .

BRYONY was sleeping peacefully. Sara sipped the cup of tea a nurse had brought her and tried to think what she would say to Robert.

No begging him to come, she told herself. No moral blackmail either, making out the situation was a lot worse than it actually was. Simply state the facts and let him come to a decision. If he'd rather stay and study, well . . .

"Sara," said a deep, familiar voice behind her.

She turned.

"Robert! How did you know? Did Jenny call you?"

He shook his head.

"I found your note, and the neighbours said they thought you'd come here. I couldn't bear to think that I had driven you away like that. I didn't even stop to pack a case. It wasn't till I reached the guest-house that I discovered you were here at the hospital. Oh, Sara, I'm so sorry."

"It's not your fault. The whole thing was an accident."

"But if there had been two of us, it might have been avoided. I could have played with Bryony while you were resting."

Robert leaned across the bed and stroked his daugher's forehead tenderly.

"How is she now?"

"She's fine. Just sleeping off the shock. They say that I can take her away when she wakes up."

"That *we* can, Sara," Robert murmured.

"You're going to stay?"

"I'm staying, if you'll have me. Oh, Sara, I shouldn't have been so stubborn and unreasonable! I'd got so caught up in that wretched struggle for promotion that I quite lost sight of why I wanted it. For you — and Bryony.

"Forgive me, please. You've no idea how terrible it felt to realise you'd gone without me. I couldn't bear to think you were happier without me."

"Never, Rob," she whispered. "Oh, never that! The only thing I discovered was how bleak my life could be. And Bryony's. She asked for you from the beginning, from the moment that we got to Jenny's.

"And when she had the accident, she cried for you as well as me. I was about to ring. Will you take us home?"

Robert slipped his arms around her.

"No. Not yet. You've booked the room. I reckon we'd be fools to waste the chance of having six whole days together, just the three of us."

"But your exams?"

"I'll cope. In fact, I'll cope far better knowing we are really close again. And if I don't . . . well, all that matters is to be a family again — and there's no written test for that."

Sara smiled.

"But if there was," she answered, reaching for his kiss, "we'd pass with flying colours now." □

LOUISE sneaked a look at her watch and thought, only ten minutes more, then you can say you've got to go . . . You've got a headache . . .

The voice droned on from the other side of the restaurant table. He seemed to have finished with cameras, now he was going into every imaginable detail about light and exposure.

Louise knew that it was her own fault. Janet, who worked in the same small office, had recently become engaged, and was eager to see everyone she knew equally happy. When Roger, Janet's fiancé, was given the task of entertaining a visitor to his firm, she had instantly seen him as a partner for her thirty-year-old friend.

After a lot of persuasion, Louise had reluctantly agreed to form a foursome. She had not expected Prince Charming, but the rather stocky thirty-something man with unruly hair who had met them at the restaurant was a disappointment all the same.

Three Cheers For Prince Charming

by SHEILA HOLROYD

GODSHILL CHURCH, ISLE OF WIGHT : J CAMPBELL KERR

David Brooks had been as nervous as she was, and over dinner they had failed to find anything in common. Janet and Roger were too absorbed in each other to notice the rapidly deteriorating situation. In desperation, as Louise became more and more silent, David had started to talk about his hobby of photography, pouring out technical details until Louise could have screamed with boredom.

Suddenly she was aware that he had stopped talking, and looked up. His anxious-to-please smile had gone, and he looked at her steadily.

"It isn't working, is it?" he said quietly.

She shook her head, now guiltily aware that the evening spent with a near-mute woman must have been as much of an ordeal for him, as it had been for her.

"Then we might as well stop now." He murmured something to Roger, and summoned the waiter with a flick of the hand.

Louise was briefly aware of the authority he must have shown in his job as field manager with an oil company in the Middle East.

"I'll take you home," David said as he ushered her out.

Eager to escape, she protested that there was no need to do that, that she would take a taxi, but he insisted.

"From what you said, I have to go near your road to get back to my hotel."

Louise sank gratefully into the luxurious darkness of the large car. At least, she thought wryly, I've had a good meal in a first-class restaurant and I'm being driven home in a comfortable car. What a pity I've hated every minute!

IT only took five minutes to reach the small terraced house where she had lived all her life. Her father had died when she was a young child, and she had been very close to her mother. It was since her death, a year ago, that Louise had become conscious sometimes of her loneliness.

The car purred to a stop, and Louise got out, muttering insincere thanks for the evening. David Brooks made similar polite noises, but he had not turned the engine off. Obviously, like her, he did not want to prolong the evening. She turned gratefully to put her key in

---

◄ p15.

GODSHILL CHURCH, ISLE OF WIGHT

THIS picture-postcard village attracts thousands of visitors every year. They are drawn to the Old Smithy, a wishing well, the Witch's brewery, a toy museum and model village and, of course, the chance to have cream teas and browse in antiques and curio shops. High above the village perches the church, Godshill's crowning glory. Legend has it that the original builders laid the foundations on a flatter, more accessible site, but every morning the stones were found on the hilltop. Eventually the builders conceded defeat and constructed the church on its commanding knoll.

---

the front door, and then gave an exclamation as it opened under her hand and silently swung inwards.

"What is it?" The sharp query from the car cut across her bewilderment.

"The door . . . It's open, and I always check carefully . . . " Her voice faded away as the possible implications of the open door struck her.

Now the car engine was turned off, and David Brooks strode purposefully to her side.

"Stay here while I check," he said, pushing the door wide and going in.

She heard the click of the light switch, and the sound of a door opening, then a muttered exclamation. Unable to wait any longer, Louise rushed in and found him in the lounge, grimly staring at utter chaos. Books and broken ornaments were strewn over the floor. Her bureau had been forced open and ink splashed on the wall.

"Call the police, while I check upstairs," David ordered crisply. By the time she had dialled and explained the situation, he had returned. She looked at his stern face.

"I'm afraid it's just as bad up there."

A glimpse of red leather caught her eye, and she gave a sudden wail, dropping to the floor to extract a photograph album from the wreckage. The sheets had been wrenched out, and the photographs were twisted and torn.

"What is it?"

"My photographs," she said numbly. "There were some pictures of Dad and my mother together. They were the only memories I had of him. Now I've nothing."

Other pictures had been torn as well, pictures of her mother as a young woman with the baby Louise, pictures taken on their rare holidays. Ornaments and books could be replaced, but the destruction of the photographs seemed to rob her of part of her life.

THE police arrived, and went methodically into action. Louise found herself huddled in an armchair, gratefully clutching a mug of hot, sweet tea that David had produced. Under questioning, she realised that only a few, easily portable, objects such as a radio and a couple of other electrical appliances had actually been taken. The wanton destruction had been the worst part.

"Not professionals," said the police sergeant. "Lads out to see what they could find . . . vandals. We'll do our best, but I'm afraid there's not much to go on. Would you like us to call a neighbour or anything?"

Louise shook her head. She felt very tired, drained. All she wanted to do was sleep. Tomorrow she would have to face the ruin of her house.

"We'll manage," David said firmly. "Now I think Louise has had enough for the night . . . "

He ushered the police out and came back to stand frowning over her. She looked up wanly.

"I'm sorry I got you involved in all this," she said, "especially after I ruined your evening."

He smiled back at her comfortingly.

"Don't worry," he said. "You should see some of the things I've coped with in the desert. Stay where you are and I'll make you another cup of tea."

Too exhausted to move, she obeyed him, and felt herself drifting off to sleep as she drank. She woke with a start when he spoke to her.

"I've put a hot water-bottle in your bed," he said practically, "so you've a warm bed to go to, but I'm afraid you've got a lot of work ahead of you tomorrow."

Too tired to speak, she stumbled up the stairs, only vaguely aware of the front door closing.

Surprisingly, she slept late the next day. It was Friday, and after telephoning the office to explain the situation and evading Janet's questions about David, she worked steadily for hours, piling what had been broken and damaged beyond redemption into binbags.

She scrubbed and cleaned steadily, keeping the washing machine busy all day. She felt as if she were cleansing the house of the intruders' presence, as well as cleaning up the physical mess they had left.

The house seemed different. Many objects which she had known all her life had vanished for good, and the ink-splashed walls meant that the lounge would need re-decorating.

She looked round with new eyes. With old associations gone, it no longer felt like home. She suddenly realised there was no reason why she should stay on here. She could move somewhere else, rent a flat and use some of the money for a good holiday . . . A thousand possibilities seemed to open up.

On Saturday she shopped for some essentials, and found time to wonder how David was. She would have liked an opportunity to thank him for his help.

Looking back on the evening, the early impression of a dull, non-descript man vanished, as she remembered his calm efficiency and the unassuming courage with which he had been prepared to deal with any lurking intruders. Her lips twitched into an involuntary smile — she was quite sure that Prince Charming would never have thought of the hot water-bottle!

DAYS passed. The house now had some semblance of normality, and Louise had already made some tentative inquiries about selling.

The following Saturday morning there was a knock at the door. Louise, busy painting the lounge walls, looked out of the window and saw a large, vaguely familiar car outside. David Brooks was at the door, holding a large parcel.

"Come in!" she welcomed him, waving a paint brush in the

direction of the kitchen.

He edged past the stepladder and paintpots in the lounge, and reached the comparative sanctuary of the kitchen, where he handed the parcel to Louise.

"Sorry I couldn't bring this before," he said simply, "but some of it was trickier than I expected."

She unwrapped the parcel while he watched. Inside was the red leather photograph album. It had been carefully repaired. Inside were Louise's photographs, as she remembered them before the burglary.

"I stuck them together and re-photographed them," he said. "I'm afraid one or two couldn't be rescued, and there are some marks visible on a few."

She gazed down at the well-remembered pictures of her parents, and felt tears brim in her eyes.

Make Yourself A Memory

MAKE yourself a memory
For the bleaker years,
Flashing like a meteor
Through a night of tears.
Happiness can be re-lived,
Songs can be re-sung.
Make yourself a memory
While your heart is young.

— Gaye Wilson.

"You've done marvellously," she said softly. "You've given my parents back to me, and I can't thank you enough."

Smiling gratefully and dressed in jeans and an old sweater spattered with paint, she seemed very different from the stiff, silent figure at the restaurant.

David relaxed and smiled back at her. She noticed how the laughter lines crinkled round his eyes, and how blue his eyes were.

"Why not let me help you some more? I'm very good with a paint brush. We could finish in a couple of hours and then go out to lunch?"

He stopped. A touch of his original nervousness returned. He laid a hand on her arm.

"I've been thinking about the other night. We made a bad start — maybe it was just because we're both a bit shy. Do you think we could try again? My firm have told me that they're taking me out of the field and posting me to New York, but I'll be here for the next few weeks."

They looked at each other. No promises, no commitments, but a new start, new possibilities . . .

Louise smiled at him.

"I've got some overalls you can borrow, " she said. "I'll find you another paint brush. And there's a very good Chinese restaurant in town." □

"It's Not

CHARLOTTE CUNNINGHAM flicked her sports car down through the gears and turned into the beech-lined driveway of one of Edinburgh's most exclusive boarding schools.

She parked in front of the pillared Georgian building and took a moment to compose herself. This morning's phone call from the school had sounded anything but routine and she was worried about her young brother.

The call had been the second bit of alarming news that day. The first was a letter from a joiner her solicitor had engaged to keep an eye on their parents' old house. Apparently, water was seeping through the roof and the joiner had sent an estimate for approval before the work was carried out.

But it wasn't the cost that had leapt out at her from the page. It was the letter heading.

CAMERON CAMPBELL: JOINER.

Charlotte had traced the first letter of his name with her finger, conscious that little shock waves were rippling backwards across her scalp.

So he was back in Kildun again . . . That the mere sight of his name could affect her so deeply after all these years was extremely disconcerting.

Resolutely, Charlotte thrust away all thoughts of Cameron Campbell. She reminded herself that she was no longer a naive teenager but the successful manageress of a chain of luxury hotels. She pinned a stray hair back into her neat bun, touched up her lipstick, and walked briskly towards the imposing oak doors.

A quarter of an hour later, she emerged, ashen-faced, from the school. Tom trailed behind her. She bundled him and his belongings into the car and sped off, spraying gravel.

by
KATE
MACLACHLAN

"Too Late"

She had always felt protective towards Tom, probably because of the fourteen-year age gap between them.

She wasn't fooled now by his blank expression — she could tell by his pallor and rigid posture that he was desperately upset.

In the end, she reached out and squeezed his hand.

"Sorry," he mumbled.

"I must know why you've been doing these things," she said calmly. But Tom didn't answer. Charlotte weaved her way through the lunch-hour traffic and pulled in at the kerb.

"Why have you been stealing?" she demanded, facing him squarely. "Were you short of money?"

"You always make sure I've got enough money."

"Why, then? Are you unhappy?"

He shrugged.

"About Mum and Dad?" she asked more gently.

For a moment she thought he wasn't going to answer, then the words came tumbling out.

"The kids kept talking about family holidays and birthday barbecues and big Christmas get-togethers — showing me photos and letters and cards. I couldn't stand it!"

Family things, she reflected. The things Tom no longer had.

Sobs shook his thin body and when she put her arm around his shoulders, he clung to her.

"I couldn't stop myself," he confided. "I couldn't stop stealing. It was awful!"

"I wish you'd told me," she said. "We could have worked something out."

"What, Charlotte? I know I can't live with you. You've got your career to think of."

GUILT crashed down on her. After their parents had been killed in a car accident two years ago, Charlotte had closed up the family home and brought Tom to live with her in Edinburgh. But her long working hours and a demanding boyfriend had made it an impossible arrangement.

One day they had sat down and talked things through.

"I'm not Mum," she'd told him. "I can't just keep house and look after you. And in years to come you'd feel guilty if I'd given up my career just for you."

Tom, then aged eleven, had agreed. Together they had found him a first-class boarding-school where they both hoped he would make new friends.

"Are we going to your poky old flat?" he asked now, wiping tears away from his freckled face.

"You mean my chic little pied-a-terre," she teased him. "In an exclusive Edinburgh enclave?"

"I want to go home, Charlotte."

"Home." She swallowed hard, recalling next week's packed diary. "You mean Kildun?"

"Of course, Kildun!" Tom said decisively.

Of course.

Tom was thirteen now. Old enough to know his own mind. He didn't want an expensive education. He wanted his old home, his old friends and no doubt his old school, too.

"OK," she said.

Tom gasped.

"You mean it?"

"Just for a few days. After all, we can't sort out your future in the middle of Princes Street!"

"But what about Nick the Nerd?"

Nick! She had forgotten all about her boyfriend. Now she remembered that he'd bought expensive tickets for a big concert that evening. Nick didn't take kindly to having his plans thwarted. He was a financial wizard who loved to make money.

"Sorry about the concert," she told his answering machine a few minutes later. "Tom's been expelled and we're going to Kildun to discuss things. I'll ring you when I get back."

Relieved that Nick had been out, she slid back into the car and grinned at Tom.

"Kildun, here we come."

CHARLOTTE was woken the next morning by a beam of sunlight reaching through the tiny bedroom window. Outside, fishermen were shouting their catches and gulls shrieked. Behind them, the tide pounded the shingle beach — a sound as reassuring as the beat of her own heart.

The sounds of home. And yet, not quite, because the cottage itself brimmed with unaccustomed silence. There was no murmur of voices from the kitchen, no echo of metal as her mother filled the kettle at the old stone sink. A tear leaked out and she brushed it away impatiently.

Two years had passed, yet she still wept every time she came back to Kildun. If a twenty-seven-year-old career girl still grieved, she could only imagine how much harder it must be for Tom.

Tom was already down on the pier, talking to one of the older fishermen, Sandy MacKay. She shouted a cheerful good morning to them from the front door and surveyed her home village with satisfaction.

Kildun was a string of higgledy-piggledy cottages pinned to the ground between crumbling sandstone cliffs and the moody North Sea. In winter, storm waters battered the shuttered windows and heavy wooden doors, but today the white-washed stone cottages sparkled like sugar lumps in the sun. It was the stuff of postcards.

Later, Charlotte opened all the windows and doors and busied herself spring cleaning. She turned out cupboards, washed down paintwork and polished furniture.

She had flung on trousers and a sweater that morning — they made a welcome change from the suits she usually wore and it was nice to

Animal Talk

THE strangest farm I chanced
upon,
I heard a pig say to a swan,
"I'm the ugliest pig in all the world
I just can't get my tail uncurled."

"Oh, please don't kick up such a
row,"
Said a lazy, sleepy cow.
"When I was born my tail was
straight,
Can't change it, now it's much too
late.

I keep it swishing every day,
It helps to keep the flies away."
"Naturally," said the horse.
"I do the same with mine, of
course."

"You needn't worry," said a sheep.
"The tail you've got is the tail you'll
keep.
But you're not ugly, you look great!
Whoever saw a pig's tail straight?"

— Helen Russell.

have a duster, instead of a briefcase, in her hands.

Now, polishing the big hall mirror, the rhythmic circling of her arm slowed as she stared curiously at her reflection. Dressed like this, and with her hair loose, it was like spotting an old friend.

"Ahem!"

"Cameron!" A deep flush shot up her neck. "So it *is* you. You *are* the joiner, I mean."

"You didn't know I was back?"

"Not until yesterday," she replied. His voice sounded just as rich she remembered.

"My solicitor forwarded your letter."

"I see." He sounded thoughtful. "You're looking well, Charlie."

She laughed, a little nervously.

"Nobody's called me Charlie for years." The truth was that she hadn't let them. She added, "I was just thinking how much I've changed."

"I wouldn't say that." His face was in deep shadow as he stood in the doorway blocking out the sun. "Still breaking hearts?" he asked.

Clumsily, she changed the subject.

"You'll have come to mend the roof, I expect?"

"Yes. If the quote's agreeable? I saw the door open and I thought I'd come over."

"The quote's fine. Thank you."

He walked past her and she saw the changes in him at once. The shy, round-shouldered uncertainty of youth had vanished. His shoulders were thrown back to the world now, his face confident, and the milky blue eyes that had once swept her off her feet had an additional shrewdness. Cameron Campbell looked even better after ten years.

"How's young Tom?" he asked, his foot on the first stair. "I saw him down on the pier."

Charlotte hesitated for a moment before she spoke.

"He's just been expelled from school, I'm afraid. For theft."

"Is that so?" Cameron shook his head sadly. "He's had a tough time. You both have."

Charlotte nodded.

"His headmaster told me that he needs a more stable home life."

Cameron looked down on her, then laughed.

"Come on, Charlie! Just how long do you think you'd be happy to stay home and polish mirrors? Playing house was never your idea of fun."

"There is a moral obligation involved!" she snapped.

"You *have* changed!"

She turned abruptly into the kitchen and heard him make his way up to the attic.

AN hour later, just as Cameron was finishing, Tom came bounding into the house.

"Sandy says Keeler's Bay is full of seals, Charlotte. Can I go and see them?"

"Certainly not! Those cliffs are terribly dangerous."

"I'll be careful!"

But Charlotte was firm.

"Not without someone who knows the cliffs. I'd take you myself but it's years since I've been up there."

"I could take him," Cameron offered quietly.

"You? But what about your work?" she asked.

"The advantage of being self-employed," he said, "is that you can choose your own hours."

"Of course. Well . . . thanks, Cameron."

"Yes!" Tom punched the air triumphantly.

"I don't see why I should miss out on the fun!" she said impulsively. "We've got a lot to discuss, Tom, but it can wait for one day. I declare today an official holiday!"

Something flickered across Cameron's face. Pleasure? Annoyance? Charlotte couldn't be sure and she packed the picnic thoughtfully while Tom and Cameron raided the shed for fishing rods.

It was a wonderful expedition. After the climb up the cliff path, and the scramble down into Keeler's Bay, they were hot and dusty and they plunged at once into the icy sea, scaring away the seals.

Afterwards, they lay on smooth slabs of rock, enjoying their picnic in the sun. They watched the seals return, bobbing up like corks in the water, then slithering awkwardly on to rocks.

Cameron took Tom fishing off the rocks and Charlotte rediscovered the luxury of a leisurely read.

SOME time later, she felt a shadow above her and realised that she had dozed off.

"It's after five," Cameron said, sitting down beside her. "We'd better think about going."

"It's been a wonderful day." She sighed.

"Aye, the weather's held."

"That wasn't what I meant. Fishing has made Tom's day," she said, gesturing towards her brother who was still down at the water's edge. "I've enjoyed it too."

"Have you?"

"Of course."

"Just like old times, Charlie?"

"Not quite." Suddenly she felt nervous. "Tom was still in a pushchair then."

"I remember it well. Very well."

Charlotte felt the silence swell between them until she couldn't bear it any longer.

"I'm sorry, Cameron," she blurted out suddenly.

"Pardon?"

"I'm sorry for the way I treated you all those years ago."

His eyes seemed to bore into her and she found that her throat was suddenly too dry to speak.

"Is that it?" he asked roughly.

She avoided his eyes and shrugged awkwardly.

"I wish *I* could shrug it off," he said, "and tell you that it didn't matter, but I'd be lying."

"There have been other girls, haven't there?" she asked cautiously.

"Of course. But no-one who . . . affected . . . me quite like you did."

"They say you always remember your first love," she said lightly.

"How reassuring!"

She looked up, shocked by the bitterness in his voice. His face was stiff with anger.

"Charlie, when you ran away from me at the dance that night, as if you couldn't bear me to touch you, I realised it was over between us."

"Oh, Cameron, I —"

"Listen!" he demanded. "I've waited a long time to say this. If you'd had the guts to tell me to my face that you wanted to finish it, I could have handled that. Even though I thought we had something pretty special, I would have coped.

"But when you wouldn't speak on the phone, Charlie, when you left Kildun without even saying goodbye, that really messed me up.

"I stayed in the village for only a few more months — hoping you'd get in touch. I couldn't bear it without you.

"When my uncle offered me an apprenticeship in Aberdeen, I jumped at the chance. I had to leave Kildun before Christmas — I didn't want to run into you when you came back to see your parents, knowing you didn't care about me.

"You treated me terribly," he said hoarsely.

"I was only seventeen! I was starting a new life in the city and I didn't know what to do. I didn't know what to say to you, or *how* to finish it. Please believe me — I never meant to hurt you."

"Well, you certainly got that one wrong, didn't you?"

Charlotte gathered the picnic things together quickly and shouted to Tom that they were going.

The day was ruined.

IT was after six o'clock when they tramped back into the village, Tom still chattering cheerfully, Charlotte exhausted by the effort of trying to maintain a friendly charade with Cameron.

Then, just when she thought things couldn't get any worse, they did.

"There's a car outside the house," Tom declared.

HIDDEN VILLAGES OF SCOTLAND

ETHIEHAVEN (Lunan Bay, Angus)

AT Ethiehaven, where the red cliffs of Angus begin their march again at the termination of Lunan Bay's three-mile strand, you are not only within a stone's-throw of the sea, you're right beside it, and your front garden is on the foreshore!

It's not everywhere you can look out of your front window and see a school of porpoises rolling past, or a fulmar-petrel gliding overhead, but that's the way of it here.

Ethiehaven has another name — Torrenshaven — not unlike Thorshaven, a Norse place name for a Scandinavian settlement. It must be added, however, that, long after the stormy days of the North Sea rovers, a family named Toren lived here in the 18th century. "Francis Torn Shipmaster" is mentioned in the old records of nearby Inverkeilor Church.

Yet, inland from Ethiehaven rises "Corbie's Knowe", where traditionally the raven-standard of the Norsemen was planted during one of their raids.

Truly a coast that bristles with tradition and legend.

"It's Nick's." She recognised his blue BMW at once. What on earth was he doing here?

Nick's slender figure emerged from the driver's seat as they approached. His hair was ruffled, his silk tie had come adrift and his shirt sleeves were rolled up above his elbows. He had clearly been waiting for some time.

"This is a fine welcome," he called. "Locked out!"

"Sorry, Nick," Charlotte replied, "but I wasn't expecting you."

He pecked her cheek and shook hands with Cameron.

"Hello, Skunk," he said to Tom.

"I suppose you've come to ruin everything," Tom growled.

"Could you two wait till we get inside before you start bickering?" Charlotte asked, fumbling for the key.

Cameron began to excuse himself. Charlotte realised that he must be as anxious to part company as she was. But Tom had other ideas.

"Please don't go," he begged. "Not yet. I *need* you here."

In the end, Cameron allowed himself to be dragged inside while Charlotte poured them all long glasses of orange juice, apologising for the lack of ice.

"It's the gin I'm missing, not the ice," Nick quipped.

"I said I wasn't expecting you," Charlotte repeated frostily.

It was Cameron who broke the silence.

"There used to be an inn here where you could buy a bottle. But after the owner died, they couldn't find anyone to take it over."

"Hardly surprising that nobody wants to move to a place like Kildun," said Nick.

Charlotte saw Cameron's hostility rise and, momentarily, she felt thrown by the increasing complexity of events. Then she took charge.

"So what brought you here, Nick?"

"I was worried."

"Worried?" she echoed.

"You don't generally drop work at a moment's notice and rush off to the end of the world."

"But you know why we're here," she reminded him. "I left a message."

"Yes. I thought you might need a hand with Skunk here."

"Don't call Tom that. And thanks for your concern, but I'm quite capable of coping with this situation myself."

"So I see," Nick said, eyeing Cameron. He turned to Tom. "What did you do to get kicked out of school?"

Tom didn't answer and eventually Charlotte murmured that one or two things had gone missing.

"Theft!" Nick spat out the word. "There are special schools for boys like you, Tom. We'll find one and then Charlotte can get back to the real world."

"Go away!" Tom yelled.

"Nick, you really aren't helping." Charlotte put her arm around Tom reassuringly. "When we find a school for Tom, it'll be one that he's happy with — no matter how long it takes."

"You're too soft on that kid!" Nick rounded on the youngster. "Your sister left this backwater ten years ago and she's gone straight to the top. That's where she belongs, not stuck here fussing round a snotty thirteen-year-old."

"That's enough, Nick." Cameron had got to his feet. He looked as if he wanted to knock the living daylights out of Nick. "I think you've said more than enough."

"You can keep out of it," Nick retorted.

"Nick!" Charlotte exclaimed. "Cameron is a friend of mine."

"A friend? You introduced him as the joiner. But then, you don't usually take tradesmen out for picnics, do you? Come to think of it, didn't you once mention a Cameron Campbell?"

"No!"

"Something about unrequited love?"

Cameron turned to stare at Charlotte.

"I really think you'd better leave," she said, furiously.

"I'm going. I can see I'm intruding." Nick paused at the door. "Sixty pounds I wasted on those concert tickets, Charlotte. Sixty!"

"I think you'd better find someone else to take to concerts," she said coldly.

THE door banged, an engine roared, and Nick screeched away.

"Nice bloke," Cameron commented. "Whatever did you see in him, Charlotte?"

"I knew he could be ruthless in business, but I've never seen him like that before."

"I have." It was Tom speaking. "But he's right, isn't he, Charlotte? You'd better find some other place to lock me up because this isn't my real home any longer. We've just been pretending today!"

Tears spilled down Tom's cheeks but Cameron stopped Charlotte following him out of the back door.

"Give him time, Charlie. Right now he needs to be alone. You can talk later."

"You're right. I'm sorry Nick was so horrible to you. He was furious about losing all that money."

Cameron shook his head.

"I don't think so."

"What?"

"He thought he might be losing you, Charlie."

"Well, he was right about that!" She paced angrily around the room. "He's never loved me. I'm just someone he likes to be seen with, an ornament for his arm, an accessory to his lifestyle — like his flashy cars and his smart suits."

"And did you love him?"

"No! He was a — a —"

"An accessory to *your* lifestyle?"

His words stopped her short. She was standing beside the window and she looked out at her sports car. She thought of her Edinburgh flat, her bulging jewellery boxes and the wardrobes stuffed with clothes. She thought of Nick and of Cameron and of the various boyfriends in between.

They stood like milestones on the road she had travelled; away from warm, chaotic love to the ultimate status symbol of a suave designer man.

Had she mistaken achievement for fulfilment?

When Charlotte turned around, Cameron had gone.

TOM returned home at nine o'clock and went straight to bed, having eaten supper with Sandy MacKay.

Charlotte dined alone on tinned soup, thinking hard. Tom meant more to her than anyone else in the world, and she was in danger of losing him as she had lost Cameron all those years ago.

She had to respect Tom's wishes, and it was clear that he wanted to stay in Kildun. Perhaps she should approach Sandy MacKay and his wife about the possibility of taking Tom as a lodger? That might be one answer to the problem. She decided to sleep on it.

But sleep eluded her. Was it just yesterday that she had woken up in Edinburgh, relishing the prospect of half a dozen business meetings and an evening out with Nick? Now, the glitzy conferences she stage-managed seemed pompous and artificial, and the parties where she socialised unutterably trivial and dull.

Everything she valued lay here. Tom, Cameron and this leaky, creaky house still suffused by her parents' love. Nothing had been quite the same since they died.

The old house sighed and creaked around her, offering its own special comfort, and she got up and crossed to the window, reassured by the sound of the waves on the shingle.

Here, in Kildun, in the middle of the night, she had somehow reached a crossroads.

Carefully, she began to assess the practicalities of working from home. Perhaps she could branch into something new. What sort of business did Kildun need?

There were several lights still shining in the village, but the old inn stood in darkness, shuttered and ponderous, as if waiting for a magician to jerk it back to life.

Charlotte felt the familiar tingle of excitement. What couldn't she bring to a place like that! She would have honeyed lights in the bar, a grand piano and logs burning in an open stove.

She would build a children's playground and have rooms for poetry readings, folk concerts and ceilidhs. A duckpond in the garden, and long trestle tables where people could linger over lagers for as long as they liked . . .

Several times, Charlotte's initiatives had stunned the world of hotel management. Well, now she would stun them again, by leaving. It wasn't too late. She would change direction, make a proper home again for Tom, and get back, at last, to being herself.

MUCH later, something woke her, some noise louder and more insistent than wind or rain. A rattle.

Someone was throwing pebbles at her window.

"Cameron!" she cried, peeping out.

"You kept me waiting once before," he called softly. "Are you going to do that again?"

She raced downstairs in her long white nightdress and when she opened the door, Cameron pulled her gently into the starry night and wrapped his rough black jacket around her shoulders.

"Unrequited?" he demanded. "Nick said *unrequited* love?"

She nodded and his eyes burned so blue and passionate that she reached up and brushed his temple with her finger.

Her hand was trembling.

"I loved you so much, Cameron. So very much. If I had stayed another minute at that dance, if I had talked to you or looked at you, or even written, then I would never have been able to leave you."

"For your precious career, you mean? . . . Then you didn't despise me, Charlie?"

"Never! I'm so sorry I hurt you, Cameron. But don't ask me to regret everything, because I can't. You see, without my training and my savings, I'd never be able to buy the old inn and renovate it the way I plan to." She was smiling and he stared at her.

"You're staying in Kildun?"

"If you don't mind. But if you never want to see me again, I'll understand. I'll take Tom and we'll start again in some other place.

"I couldn't bear to stay here with you hating me as much as you seemed to on the cliffs today."

He answered by taking her in his arms and she inhaled that blend of salt and wood and oil that was for ever Cameron.

When their lips met, gentle and caressing, she knew that this was the kiss she had been wanting for ten long years.

"I love you," he murmured. "I always have . . ."

"Me too." She nuzzled lovingly against him, reaching up for his kiss. □

Married Bliss

MARRIED bliss can
Come to grief,
In unsuspected
Small ways.
These fatal phrases
Pave the way . . .
You never *and*
You always*!*

— Gaye Wilson.

KATE fumed with impatience as the blue Renault continued its steady fifty miles an hour in the centre lane. The fast lane was crowded, so there was no chance of overtaking it.

She glowered at the back view of the driver — selfish, inconsiderate idiot. Where did he think he was? It was eight o'clock on a Monday morning on the *motorway*, for goodness' sake.

She considered flashing her lights, then took another quick look in the rear mirror. Three . . . four cars coming up fast, then a gap. With immaculate timing she made her manoeuvre and was once more free to press ahead.

She turned slightly and glimpsed an elderly lady at the wheel of the Renault, sitting bolt upright and composed, and immediately felt ashamed of her impatience. She reminded Kate of her mother . . . Though Hannah was no driver.

With thoughts of Hannah, anxiety came flooding back. Why hadn't she answered her telephone this morning? She'd an extension by her bed. After repeated attempts to reach her

HER RIGHT TO CHOOSE

there had been no alternative but to drive over.

She'd been in the kitchen dishing up the spaghetti last night when the telephone rang.

"I'll get it," she'd called, knowing that if either of the girls answered they could be gossiping away for ages and the meal spoiled.

"That you, Kathy? This is Mrs Edwards."

Kate racked her brains. Kathy was her childhood name.

"Hello?" the voice persisted. "It's Mrs Edwards, your mother's neighbour, from across the road."

Her heart lurched. It was "the Crow" — the nickname the girls had produced; with her beady eyes, hooked nose and air of perpetual gloom, it suited her well.

"Is something wrong?" Kate asked sharply. "Is it Mother?"

"I thought you ought to know," the voice continued, "she's had a fall . . . Not that she'll thank me for telling you."

Kate felt her knees grow weak and she sank down on the stairs.

"What happened? Is she all right?"

"Well, it's hard to say. I'd just called round with the parish magazine and there she was, all bruised. Said she'd had a bit of a tumble . . . I blame that cat, not that she'd hear a word against him."

Greg came into the hall, and she mouthed, "It's Mother."

"Has she had the doctor?" she asked Mrs Edwards.

"No — you know what she's like . . . have to be on her death bed. Well, I couldn't do anything right, she sends me off to fetch Charlie."

She would, Kate thought distractedly. Solid, dependable Charlie whose wife had died about the same time as Kate's father. He and her mother had supported each other ever since.

by
ANNA
BRAMWELL

"I'll ring her right away," she said.

"Won't do you no good. She'll have taken her hearing aid out. I noticed her bedroom light go off a while ago."

"Then I'll have a word with Charlie."

"You'll be lucky. Sits there all evening with them earphones on listening to his music . . . oblivious to anything else."

She'd been right. Kate tried time and again to get through, but there was no response from either phone. She wanted to drive over there and then, but Greg persuaded her it was more sensible to wait till morning.

THERE had been little sleep that night. After years of seeming to be indestructible, Hannah was beginning to decline. She was becoming more and more forgetful and this would be the second fall she'd had recently that Kate knew about. What was to be done? How could she keep a watchful eye on her so far away? Perhaps they ought to think about her coming to live with them.

She could have Sara's room now that she was at university. Alison and Rachel would have to share again, but they'd understand. They loved their gran.

They always said she was such fun. She used to play Monopoly for hours with them, stacking up houses, hotels and railway stations with whoops of glee.

She showed them how to play rummy, crib, whist, pontoon and ten different kinds of patience. She taught them all the old country names of wild flowers . . . They treated her as if she was one of them.

At least they had, until recently. Now when she came to stay, Kate noticed they were less exuberant, almost protective towards her.

This morning, just as she was about to leave, Alison had come running across the lawn, her feet wet from the heavy dew, and thrust a mass of white lilac into the car.

"Gran's favourite," she panted. "Give her our love."

The fragrance was filling the car.

She drew in a heady breath as she watched for her exit point from the motorway.

It was a relief to be on a minor road. In ten minutes she'd be there. She hoped the girls had got off in good time for school. Greg would be on his way to the station.

He'd not hesitated this morning at breakfast when she'd asked him what he thought of having Hannah come to live with them.

"If that's what she wants," he said amiably. "It'd save you worrying about her up there."

Why had that irked her a bit? She should have been grateful for such an understanding husband.

But then, he wouldn't be at home with her all day. Kate would have to give up her part-time work — Hannah wouldn't take kindly to being left on her own.

And Kate loved her job at the bookshop; she loved the smooth feel of the paper, the smell of the bindings, the attractive covers. The shop, in the narrow back street off the market square, seemed to welcome her when she arrived in the mornings. She loved being a part of it, it would be a wrench to give it up.

No. Kate knew that it wasn't going to be easy. Hannah liked to do things her way.

Whenever she came to visit, Kate would plan the meals in advance; spaghetti, lasagne, things they all liked were out.

"Can't stand that foreign rubbish." Hannah would stand sniffing at a casserole. "There's no garlic in that, is there?"

She'd follow Kate around, switching off lamps in the evening.

"You don't want all these on, such a waste."

She expected to watch all her favourite TV programmes — snooker, racing, wrestling and most of the soaps — and innocently assumed they'd all sit and watch together.

"Where are you off to now?" she'd ask, aggrieved, if Kate tried to slip off upstairs with a book.

After she'd gone home — and she'd never stay more than a couple of weeks because Sam, her ginger cat, would fret — Kate would turn the TV screen to the wall. She'd have afternoons of blissful window shopping and emerge from the library with armfuls of books, and go round turning on lamps and reclaiming her home once more.

But then she'd be consumed with guilt. How could she feel this way, when she really loved her mother?

Now, as she turned into the familiar road, she noticed a curtain twitch at "the Crow's" house, just as it had a year ago when Kate arrived for her father's funeral.

THERE was a familiar sound as she approached the kitchen door — the swish-thump of a twin tub. Of course, it was Monday.

A puff of steam eddied out of the open window as Kate peered in. There Hannah stood, in her blue pinafore, her grey hair frazzled from the steam, bundling wet clothes into the spin dryer.

"Mum," Kate said softly from the doorway.

Hannah spun round, startled.

"Kate!" she exclaimed, rubbing her misted spectacles with the corner of her apron. "Is that you? Whatever brings you . . .?"

"Don't I get a hug?"

Kate crossed the floor and pressed her face to her mother's soft cheek.

"Let me have a look at you," Kate said and gently turned her mother's face towards the light, revealing a large area of discolouration over the right temple. "What have you been up to?"

"How did you know?" Hannah asked truculently, then drew back in indignation. "No. Don't tell me, I know. Mrs-can't-mind-her-own-business-Edwards from across the road. Rang you, did she?"

"Just as well," Kate said defensively, "otherwise I'd never have known."

Hannah's tongue clicked in annoyance.

"Such a fuss over a silly fall. It's these new bi-focals, I'm not used to them yet. But that's no reason for you coming all this way, leaving your husband and the girls. Why didn't you ring?"

"I *did* ring. I rang last night, I rang this morning. Time and again but you never answered. I was so worried, I had to come."

"Oh, lovey." Hannah's face crumpled with remorse. "My hearing aid. I must've upset something in it when I fell. Charlie had a look at it this morning and managed to fix it. Oh, I *am* sorry putting you to this bother."

"It's no bother, Mum. But don't you think the doctor should have a look at you?"

"Oh, stop your hassle, Katie. I'm as good as new. Now, let me get this washing out of the way and we'll settle down for a good chat before you have to get back."

Kate was surprised. She'd planned to stay the night at least, but she wouldn't argue about that now.

She fetched the lilac from the car and arranged it in a cut glass vase. Then, whilst Hannah went out to the clothes line, she started to unload the spin dryer. She was holding aloft a man's vest and pyjamas in the big wooden tongs when her mother returned.

"What's this, then?" she asked. "You taking in laundry, or have

HIDDEN VILLAGES OF SCOTLAND

COTTOWN (St Madoes)

IF you turn southwards from the Perth — Dundee highway at Glencarse, you will soon come within the spell of St Madoes and that delightful old-world village of Cottown.

Notice I said "soon," yet the brief side-step takes you back through the years to the 11th century, for here is the ancient Hawk Stane linked with the Battle of Luncarty and that historic family, Hays of Errol.

Cottown is quite near, and wandering through the village you find the metalled road dwindling to a track, then losing itself near the reedy shores of the Tay, directly opposite Newburgh.

The cottages are thatched and picturesque, each with its colourful flower garden. Older still are several

houses partly built of clay, dating back to the 17th century.

Cottown was once more self-supporting than now. It had its joiner, smith, grocer, tailor and school-ma'am. Making use of material from a nearby quarry, it "exported" bricks and tiles.

In fact, it lay in a world of its own — still does to some extent. Noticeably quiet and pleasing, after the frantic major roads!

you got a lodger?"

"Now just leave them be." Hannah plucked the tongs from her. "They're a few things of Charlie's I slip in at the end. Saves him a trip to the launderette." She put them in a bowl at her side.

"It's no bother to me," she said defensively, "with all this soapy water. You can keep on adding things with a twin tub. Not like that fancy washing machine of yours, wasting good suds."

"You'll have your neighbours talking," Kate teased.

"Don't give them the chance," Hannah said tartly. "Charlie hangs them on his own line."

Kate looked at her mother with affection, at the raised chin and the stubborn mouth.

"I'm sure he's grateful," she said appeasingly.

"He gives as good as he gets," Hannah said, making a neat pile of Charlie's washing. "Keeps my garden tidy, drives me around when I need it. We look out for each other in these parts. You should know that, Katie."

IT was then that Kate began to wonder how Hannah would feel about moving away. Guiltily, she realised she'd not been considering it from her point of view at all. All the time she helped clear up the kitchen and lay the table for lunch she pondered how best to bring it up.

She kept up a bright chatter about the girls and the things they'd been doing as they ate and Hannah listened and laughed. But after they'd eaten and were sitting over a glass of wine, Hannah spoke.

"Come on, out with it. Whatever it is that's on your mind. Let's be having it."

Kate looked at her mother across the table — the shrewd blue eyes, the freckled hands, and the purple bruise so vivid on the delicate skin.

"I do worry about you, Mum." Her voice thickened. "This is the second fall you've had recently."

Hannah's eyes twinkled impishly.

"Two falls and a submission!" She grinned. "Don't worry, they'll not be counting me out just yet."

"It's no joke, Mum. You don't tell me things. If Mrs Edwards . . ."

"Do *you* tell *me* things?" Hannah broke in. "When you found that lump — if Rachel hadn't let it slip, would I have known?"

"It was only a cyst."

"But you didn't know till later. You going through all that and me not knowing. How do you think I felt?"

"I didn't want to worry you."

"There you are, then. That makes two of us."

Kate's fingers traced a circle in the tablecloth.

"If only you were nearer . . ." she murmured. "Mum, we wondered . . ." She hesitated, then the words came out in a rush.

"We'd really like it if you'd come and live with us. You could have Sara's old room and I'd make it specially nice for you. Greg said I was to ask you, and you know how the girls would love it. Will you think about it?"

Hannah sat upright in her chair, then pulled herself to her feet and busied herself carrying plates and dishes to the sink. When she turned round her eyes were bright. She came over and put her hands on Kate's shoulders.

"I'm touched you should ask me, lovey," she said. "You're a lovely daughter. But it'd never do. Why, the very idea! How could I leave Charlie and all my friends? And Sam — why, he'd die of shock! Like me, he's far too old to transplant."

"But I'd like to take care of you, if . . ."

"Do I look as if I need caring for?" Her shoulders stiffened. "And if the time comes . . . Well, look at Ivy down the road — not left the house for donkeys' years, yet she knows more of what's going on than I do.

"Home help, meals on wheels, community nurse . . . they all come, even chiropodist and hairdresser. You don't have to be stuck fast these days. Besides —" She splashed water in the sink and squirted in the detergent. "You know what I've always said. Two women in a kitchen will never get on."

"There'd be no need for you . . ."

"Now that's where you're wrong, Katie. Can you see me sitting around, twisting my fingers? I'll keep my independence for as long as I can, thank you. But bless you for your offer."

She peered into her daughter's face. "Don't look so bothered. What's an odd fall, now and then? I'll take my chance. That's the way I want it. It's my choice."

THE light was just beginning to fade as Kate left the motorway. The return journey had none of the compulsion of the morning's one.

Hannah had insisted she get back to Greg and the girls, and Kate hadn't demurred. She'd slipped round to see "the Crow" and Charlie while her mother took in her washing.

It was Charlie who revealed they were going to a whist drive later. Her heart warmed at her indomitable mother, who brushed away falls and mishaps like troublesome flies, refusing to let them alter her life one jot.

Kate smiled ruefully. She'd gone rushing up there to take over Hannah's problems and sort out her life. But her mother had made it quite clear that she was still in charge, and had a perfect right to choose the way she wanted to live.

Kate had to accept that. But she'd also extracted a promise from Charlie and "the Crow" to let her know if she was needed, and she resolved to telephone and visit her more often.

Hannah's parting words came back to her as she pulled up outside her own home.

"You'll be just like me when you're my age. Stubborn to the end!"

Kate smiled. She did hope so . . . □

by CERI EVANS

ONE STEP AT A TIME

JUST two minutes, Mike," the nurse said softly. "Although I hardly need to tell *you* that."

"I promise I won't stay," he whispered. "But I simply had to come. You understand?"

"Yes, of course, but if Sister catches us . . ."

"I'll defend you to the death!" He went through the screens round the bed.

The girl was lying flat, as if asleep. Her skin was paler than the sheets, translucent almost, and her hair, brushed loosely back, was barely tinged with gold.

Round her there was colour he'd rather not have seen — brilliant displays of red and green on a bank of monitors.

The nurse reached out and touched her hand.

"Helen, you've a visitor."

The lashes fluttered for a moment, then the blue eyes opened.

"You won't remember me," he said.

"I don't remember anything." She sighed.

"This is Mike," the nurse said reassuringly. "He was the paramedic in the ambulance. He held your hand while they cut you out."

She blinked, trying to focus on his face.

"Then if it hadn't been for you . . ."

"My job," Mike said. "I'm only sorry it was necessary. Anyway, you're on the mend, thank goodness."

The cheerful words belied his deep anxiety, for Helen wasn't off the danger list yet.

"Perhaps you'd let me come again?"

The blue eyes lit up for a moment, then seemed to fade to grey before they closed.

Sometimes, Mike mused, his was a lousy job. The satisfaction he got from saving people barely compensated for seeing them in pain.

Maybe he should have stayed away today, but Helen had been special, brave beyond belief through all the waiting while they cut her from the car. The only sign of what she'd been going through had been the pressure of her fingers gripped round his. He couldn't forget that.

★ ★ ★ ★

It was a week before Mike ventured up into the ward again, a week when he'd worked mechanically, battling to keep his thoughts from Helen. The nurses had been wonderful, of course, keeping him up to date on her condition.

It was quite unprofessional to feel like this about a patient. He should be concerned, yet detached. But Helen's fingers had somehow touched a soft spot . . .

He shouldn't have been so absurdly happy, either, when Sister said he could visit in his tea-break, but he was singing as he took the stairs in threes.

Helen had been moved into the open ward, and there was a hint of pink about her cheeks.

"You're looking so much better," Mike said, as he laid his roses on the bed.

"I'm sorry?"

She was gazing up at him in obvious bewilderment, and he smiled a little awkwardly.

"Of course, you won't remember me. I'm . . ."

"Oh yes!" she said. "You must be Mike. The sister told me you'd be coming up some time. She told me that you'd been before, but I'm afraid I can't recall . . .

"I know I've got a lot to thank you for. Well, everything, in fact. Including these," she added, burying her face among the scented petals.

"A little celebration. And besides, I gather that you aren't having other visitors."

"That's what comes of having an accident when you've moved half across the country for a teaching post and term's just finished," she said ruefully. "My sister's got little ones, pre-school age — she can't just drop everything to come and see me."

Mike traced the pattern on the bedspread with his finger tip. "As you're on your own — " he cleared his throat, not looking at her " — I could come up at tea-break every day, if you like."

His heart thumped painfully in the ensuing silence.

"I couldn't put you to so much trouble," Helen protested thoughtfully.

"It's no trouble," Mike said eagerly. "I would be in the canteen anyway. And, with half an hour free, I could slip out if you had any errands . . ."

"I've everything I need, except a bit of company."

Mike glowed inside.

"I only wish I could come at the proper time and have an hour and a half, but I'm on evening shifts."

"I know." She smiled. "Or else we'd never have met!"

Next day Sister drew him aside.

"You've scored a hit there, Mike," she said. "She was terribly depressed before, but yesterday she showed the first real sparks of life. Once you'd gone, she asked a nurse to help her with her hair, then she bought herself some make-up from the mobile shop."

"That's great!" Mike beamed.

"We-ell, yes. But . . ."

"But what?"

"I've been nursing long enough to see the dangers. It wouldn't be the first time a member of the staff had flirted with a pretty patient."

Mike reddened and started to protest.

"You're going to tell me this is different, of course. I wish I had a pound for everyone who'd said those very words.

"There's something artificial about this situation, don't forget. It's very flattering when a pretty girl is so grateful, but in here, they've often no-one else to lean on.

"She's very vulnerable, Mike. I wouldn't like to see her hurt. She's suffering enough already, and there's more to come."

"I wouldn't . . ."

"Just be sure you don't. Lift her up too high, and there isn't any way of letting her down lightly."

Mike wandered sombrely along the corridor. Sister had a point. He owed it to Helen to explore his motives carefully. Yet, when his eyes met hers . . . It *was* quite different, this time.

"THEY got me out of bed this morning," she announced a few days later.

"That's wonderful!"

"Only as far as a wheelchair, though."

"Still, it's a step . . ." Mike stopped, and cursed himself. There could have been no worse choice of word.

"I think the steps will take a while!" she joked, then lapsed into uneasy silence, toying with the ribbon on his box of sweets.

"There's something wrong," he prompted.

"Too much time to think, probably," she answered slowly. "I just keep wondering if I'm ever going to drive again."

He hesitated. Did she realise there was a chance she might not even walk?

"You see, I think I've lost my nerve. My mother used to say that accidents don't happen, they're caused. I must have been to blame."

Relief swept over him. He wasn't sure he would have known how to cope if she had asked about her injuries, but dealing with the crash was easier.

He listed all the reasons for her. She'd been on an unfamiliar road, the corner had been blind, so she'd been driving slowly, there was no way she could have seen the oil spill till she went into a skid . . .

"Don't forget," he added, "the police measured out the tyre marks. You couldn't be more innocent. The guilty party is the one whose car was leaking, and they'll never trace him now."

"So the crash was sheer bad luck?"

That, Mike reflected, was an understatement.

"For you, but," he added lightly, "good for me. I'd not have met you otherwise."

"Beast!" She laughed. Then she frowned slightly. "I'm just a nuisance to you, really."

"Oh no," he said. "Not ever."

They sat in silence until a junior nurse came round to tidy Helen's sheets.

"It's such a glorious day," he said, when they were on their own again. "You're missing all the fun in here. Now that you're up, how would a picnic appeal to you? We've got very pretty grounds outside this building, you know."

"Your tea-break's hardly long enough for outings, Mike."

"Oh, but I've time off next week. We could be outdoors all day long."

"You ought to take the chance to get away."

Mike grinned.

"I can't quite put my finger on it, but something's keeping me here! Besides, fresh air might sharpen up your appetite. I'm told you hardly eat enough to feed a sparrow, and that's never going to get you well."

Helen wrinkled up her nose.

"Even starving sparrows wouldn't relish hospital cuisine!"

"Suppose I brought a hamper full of — well, you name it. Chicken, salmon, rare roast beef, assorted salads, melons, strawberries and pineapple?"

"Oh, stop! I'll never face the shepherd's pie tonight!"

Sister pursed her lips as Mike appeared in her office.

"I couldn't help hearing," she said. "You're wanting my permission?"

Holiday Memories

THE folded hills that fade from view
Against the sky;
The dancing harebell's hazy blue
On cliff-top high —

White cotton-grass and orchis rare
'Mid wastes of peat,
Where wild bog-myrtle fills the air
With fragrance sweet —

Bright drifts of shells where silver sands
Meet turquoise tides,
And lonely, curlew-haunted strands
Where peace abides —

Brown burns that leap from mountain height
To glen below,
And limpid lochs that catch the light
Of sunset's glow —

When "we in dreams behold" again
These lovely things,
Memory weaves her spell — and then
The glad heart sings!

— Brenda G. Macrow.

"Please. Sister. It would make such a change for her."

"I can't refuse the girl a treat. And there's no denying that you're good for her morale. But —" she added in a warning tone.

"I'll take good care of her," Mike interrupted. "There'll be no broken hearts."

"I wish I could believe you. It's getting harder for her every day, you know. Next week we're trying her on crutches. She'll need all her emotional energy to concentrate on that."

A WEEK later, Mike slipped into Sister's office.

"Did Helen manage on the crutches?"

"She tried."

There was a heavy silence.

"But will she be all right?" he blurted out.

"It's early days, but, if she perseveres, perhaps . . . Right now she's terribly depressed again."

Being in the ward all the time was bound to make her sad, he thought. In the garden, she had been so bright, so full of hope and courage . . . and, when he'd pressed his lips to hers, he'd tasted there such a zest for life. Helen wasn't born to be a cage-bird.

★ ★ ★ ★

"You've been walking," he said cheerfully.

"I stood," she whispered. "For a moment. But I couldn't move forward." She sighed. "Things don't look very good, Mike, do they? The doctors don't say much, but I can read it in their eyes."

"Nonsense. You're just feeling down. It's early days. If you persevere . . ."

She raised her troubled face.

"That's just what Sister says. I hoped that you, at least, would have the courage to be honest with me."

Mike drew a deep breath.

"You're the one with courage, Helen. I felt it in your hands, that dreadful night. And in your kiss . . ."

She looked away despondently.

"I can't believe there's a future any more," she said. "Not the one I want."

"And what about the one *I* want?"

"I'd be no good to you like this," she said. "No good at all."

A fortnight passed, and Helen got no closer to that first and crucial step. Mike racked his brains for some incentive but came up with nothing, till, one Saturday, walking through the shopping precinct to the florist's, his eye was caught by a window display he'd seen every day for weeks. This time, the idea hit him straight away.

Half an hour later he was sprinting along the corridor to Helen's ward.

He stared in horror at her empty bed, as Sister hovered at his side.

"I'm sorry, Mike, but she's discharged herself."

"She couldn't have! She's not fit enough."

"Her sister came for her. They left for Leeds this morning."

"But that's a hundred miles away!"

She shrugged.

"I told you this would end in tears."

"Is there a message for me?"

"There's a note."

MIKE'S hands were tight on the steering wheel, his knuckles white. How could she go without an explanation, without the prospect of a meeting? If Sister hadn't left Helen's file on her desk and found an errand in the ward, he wouldn't even have known where to find her.

How could Helen say she was no good for him? How could she let depression get the better of the feelings he was sure lay deep in her heart?

He pulled into a lay-by to check the street map. He traced the route to Barton Drive in pencil, propped the map against the dash and headed resolutely on.

The sound of women's voices drifted through the fence of Number 30.

"You've got to stand, Helen. You did it in hospital, and if I'd realised you wouldn't try for me, I'd never have agreed to bring you home."

"I'm sorry, Mary." Helen sobbed. "But there's no point. I watched the doctors in their huddles and I saw them studying me. It's no use. What's the point?"

"Oh, Helen, don't you understand that no-one's perfect? Love settles for the good and disregards the little flaws. If Mike loves you —"

Mike pushed open the gate.

"Love does a whole lot more than that." He smiled into Helen's startled eyes. "It drives a hundred miles to take you back for mending." He knelt down beside her chair.

"But if I can't be mended?" He saw the fear in her eyes.

"Everything about your case suggests you can, with time. The doctors don't want to raise your hopes too fast, that's all. Nobody meant to crush them, Helen." He kissed her.

"Too fast!" She drew back. "Is three months too fast?"

"It may be three months more, but you'll do it. Besides, what's three months when we've all our lives ahead of us? I'd wait for ever, if you made me."

"Perhaps you didn't tell her that before," Mary said. "Not loud enough. Once Helen's got a notion in her head, she's so stubborn . . ."

"I could shout it from the rooftops to convince you," Mike suggested, "but I'd rather promise it in church."

Helen gazed at him incredulously.

"Look," Mike said, fishing in his pocket for a tiny box. "I've chased you up the motorway with this."

Helen watched as he revealed the sparkling diamond.

"Well, aren't you going to try it?" Mike asked impatiently. "If the ring fits, you're the girl. If it doesn't, we can have it altered, but you're still the girl."

"It's perfect!" Helen gasped, and he got to his feet. Behind the chair, he could see Mary, tears in her eyes, holding her breath as he held out his hands to her sister.

"Right, then, hold my hands. Tight, now. Forward — and up!"

Falteringly, Helen rose.

"Brave girl. Now close your eyes and tell me you can see the altar 'way ahead," he said, laughing.

"I can," she breathed.

"And I can see you walking down the aisle." He cradled her in his arms, and kissed her hair. "Still think we can't mend you?"

Helen leaned her head against his shoulder.

"You'd better take me back," she murmured. "There's something Sister ought to see."

"That you want to walk?"

"No." She laughed. "My ring!" □

HIDDEN VILLAGES OF SCOTLAND

CHAPELTON CROSSROADS

CHAPELTON (locally pronounced "the Chippleton") has had several names.

Once it was Whitfield, suggesting an oasis of farmland in the midst of moorland.

Then the Earl of Southesk's family of nearby Kinblethmont established a walled garden and private burial ground with a chapel — hence the name Chapelton.

Nearer our own times, J. B. Salmond gave the "placie" the name of "Cargie" in his novel "The Toby Jug." Dr Salmond was editor of the "Scots Magazine" and a prolific writer.

A patch of grass alongside the "Cargie Crossroads" in my drawing was a favourite one-night stand with tinker families. These were the old-time "tinks" who moved around both Lowlands and Highlands — the men mending pans and making baskets, heather-besoms and scrubbers, and playing the bagpipes at Feeing-market fairs, the women selling sprays of "lucky white heather" and telling fortunes.

These old-time tinkers — so different from the highly motorised travelling people today — have left their mark in the folklore of this district near Friockheim.

The "Cargie Crossroads" form a historic point in the long saga of the tinkers' traditional routes and wanderings.

The Farmer And His Wife

by John Taylor

CAN you remember events, say, ten or even twenty years ago, yet if someone asked what you did last Thursday you might have difficulty in remembering?

I once bought Anne a recipe book. I saw it in a shop window in Cupar and on the spur of the moment I went in and bought it. The title, "Soups and Starters," I learned, meant the first course.

Well, Anne had gone to a WRI meeting in the village and had left the book on the kitchen table.

I picked it up, as I enjoy reading short stories and recipe books. Odd, I know . . .

I was browsing through the egg section when I came across curried eggs. Anne says I would add curry and onions to any dish if she'd let me!

Well, here was a recipe which used both. Just my cup of tea, but it made me think of an incident perhaps twenty or maybe thirty years previous.

It was a Tuesday and I was in Cupar for the mart, when I ran into Provost Scott of Elie.

The Provost and his good lady were friends of ours.

"Have you had lunch, John?"

"No, I was just going for a bowl of soup."

"Join me at the Royal, John — my treat."

When we sat down at a table, he ordered curried chicken and, as I like curry, I ordered the same.

A waitress brought us our curried chicken plus knives and forks.

"Miss, can we have two dessert spoons, please?" the Provost asked.

In his younger days, he had spent time in the East.

Curry was one of the staple diets out there, he pointed out, and you must always eat it with a spoon.

TO come back to curried eggs. I knew Anne wouldn't be back from the WRI meeting for ages.

When at last she came into the kitchen, she sniffed the air.

"What have you been up to, John?"

There was a smell of both onion and curry.

"Nothing, dear."

What a white lie — and she knew it.

I'd been trying out the recipe for curried eggs. It said one small onion — I always believe in whatever it says about onions to double the amount.

It said four tablespoonfuls of sultanas, but I thought they would still be hard if they hadn't been soaked overnight, so I added some chutney.

Then I'd cut the eggs in half — and put them in one of Anne's oven-proof dishes and poured the curry mixture on top.

I'll be honest, I was really pleased with my curried egg dish.

Now, don't forget — next time you have curry, all the best people eat it with a spoon.

And remember to double the onions in any recipe!

by MAY MARSHALL

Melody of Love

AILIE'S room in the convalescent home was large and airy, with a big window looking out over the promenade and the lively waters of the firth. Her dressing-gown lay neatly at the foot of one of the twin beds. The other was empty.

She sat down by the open window, pushing the white hair back from her brow with a great sigh of relief. At last she was free to be quiet, to sit in silence. Perhaps now the long nightmare of the crash and the months in hospital would recede.

She half-smiled, remembering how, in her early drugged delirium, the cheerful babble in the big busy ward had sometimes sounded like the old familiar calling of the gulls round the headland at home. Even the regular swish of the mop over the polished floor had reminded her of the comforting sounds of the great winds through the trees behind the house.

But always she'd had to wake, to the knowledge, like a heavy stone on her heart, that David was dead.

And, always, at the first waking, there had been the red blur against the snow, the flash of light and the sound of rending metal.

Now it was summer. The thought of all those lost months sent her into an unreasoning panic that brought her quickly to her feet.

She limped off to the day room and opened the door on a cheerful buzz of conversation as her fellow-convalescents waited for coffee time.

There, by the window, neatly smoothed hair showing some of its original fiery red, round face smiling a welcome, was her friend, Ann Fowler.

"It's yourself, Ailie. I was hoping you'd be down. What have you been doing?"

"Just enjoying being alone in my room." Ailie settled herself comfortably by her friend.

Ann studied her for a moment.

"You look more rested already," she said at last.

"Well, my room-mate was a fine cheery body, but she did talk all the time!"

Ann laughed. "Never mind, your son will be in to see you later."

"That's right. With John being in the Middle East, Nicol does all the visiting."

When the coffee trolley arrived, they sat in companionable silence as they ate the delicate home-made biscuits and drank their coffee.

"Mmm, delicious!" Ann said as she laid her cup aside. "You'll be glad you'd time for coffee before Doctor Wayne arrives."

"Oh, he's been," Ailie told her brightly. "He came first thing."

"And was he pleased with you?"

"Er — yes, quite pleased." Ailie fidgeted with her coffee spoon. "But he says he can't let me go home yet."

Ann looked surprised. "Why not? You're looking much better, your fractures have mended well. Surely you could convalesce just as well at home now?"

Ailie sighed. "I think so, but he says that my house is too isolated — and I suppose he's right. My nearest neighbour is a mile away on the other side of the bay."

Ann mused for a moment and then looked thoughtfully at Ailie. "Couldn't you stay with your son for a while?"

"Yes, of course I could. But, Ann, I'm just longing to go home, to be in my own house, to try to come to terms with a new way of life.

"I can't do that in someone else's home. Bay House is where my life with David began, and it's where I must learn to accept that it's over."

"I see what you mean," Ann said thoughtfully. "Did you tell Doctor Wayne how you felt?"

"Yes, I did, and he sympathised, but he was adamant and —"

Just then, Ailie felt a touch on her shoulder and turned to find the receptionist beside her.

"Sorry to interrupt, Mrs Douglas, but your son is here. I've put him in your room so you'll be able to have a chat in peace."

AILIE found Nicol standing by the open window of her room, his foot tapping idly to the music of a radio playing in some nearby room.

Just for a moment it seemed that the young David stood before her. The springing fair hair, the strong chin, the broad shoulders, all these were his father's.

GARINISH ISLAND, COUNTY CORK, EIRE

SET at the head of Bantry Bay, the shores of Garinish Island are swept by the Gulf Stream, which allows palm trees and subtropical plants to prosper. Easily reached by boat from Glengarriff, the island is home to beautiful Italian gardens. Bequeathed to the Irish people in 1953, this delightful isle is reputed to be where George Bernard Shaw wrote "St Joan".

GLENGARRIFF, COUNTY CORK : J CAMPBELL KERR

"Ma! How are you? Come and sit down." He beckoned her to a chair.

Ailie smiled. "Oh, I'm better. Much better, Nicky. How are Julie and the boys?"

"They're fine. The boys are full of mischief, as usual, and everyone sends their love. They wanted to come with me, but I thought we'd have a chat on our own."

Ailie looked up at him. "You've been talking to Doctor Wayne."

He smiled. "We never could fool you, could we?"

His face became serious and he took her hand in a tender clasp.

"You know he won't let you go back to Bay House? He feels that the accident, losing Dad, all those injuries — well, he thinks it's strained your heart a little bit.

"You can't live alone, and you should be taking things a little more easily now."

Ailie looked at him with love, grateful for the lie.

"Oh, Nicky," she said at last. "Isn't it a business? Those boys in their little red car — all in a moment they've taken my husband, my home, my health, everything."

He put his arm round her, conscious of her slightness, her frailty. "No, no, Ma! You have us — John and me, Julie and the boys."

"And I'm grateful and glad of all of you, Nicky, you know that. It's just that Dad and I were too close for too long."

"We'll help you. You'll come and be with us where we can look after you. It won't be the same, but at least we'll try to make you happy again."

As she struggled to find words to answer him, it seemed that the sound of a nearby radio became louder, until the lively dancing beat seemed to fill the room.

She gave a little gasp. "Listen, Nicky. Do you recognise it? Your dad always loved that tune. He said he couldn't keep his feet still when he heard it. Remember?"

For a moment he was bewildered by the sudden switch from the present to the past, but then his face brightened.

"Yes, of course I do. I can remember the two of you dancing in the kitchen at home!"

"He just loved to dance. And so did I." She shook her head sadly. "That's what's gone, Nicky. That feeling of being young together."

She smiled. "It didn't really matter how old we became, for we were always still pretty Ailie Asher dancing with her young man."

Her voice was full of grief as she went on, "But now he's gone. I'm Mother or Grandma, but I'll never be David's love again. It's as if, suddenly, I've been moved on . . ."

Nicky shook his head.

"You're wrong, Ma. You're not old, and you'll always be David's love. Don't you know that?"

For a moment they were a little uncomfortable with each other, but then he hugged her gently.

"Now, will you listen, Ma? Julie and I would really like you to come and live with us. I know it's not what you want, but you'd be safe and comfortable — and loved. The boys — well, you know they'd be deliriously happy to have you there every day!"

Ailie was horrified.

"Nicky, I couldn't. What an upheaval in your house! One of the boys would have to give up his room to me, and I'm far too fond of Julie to saddle her with a mother-in-law about her feet all day and every day."

She patted his hand lovingly. "But bless you both for thinking of it."

NICKY gave her a huge hug, smiling a little to himself. "That's exactly what we knew you'd say, so when John telephoned last night, we worked out a splendid plan." He laughed. "In fact, we're making you an offer you can't refuse!"

She was bewildered. "What are you talking about? What plan?"

"Well, you know the side of our house that looks down over the fields to the village? We plan to build a small extension there. It'll be just a little sitting-room, a bedroom, a shower room and a tiny galley kitchen, but it'll be yours! You can have your own garden, too."

He looked at her anxiously. "Say you'll consider it, Ma. It won't be Bay House, but you know, people are more important than places.

"You'll be with your own folk — and John can sleep easy at nights knowing you're being looked after. You don't realise how worried he's been, away out there, not able to help."

He caught sight of his watch. "Heavens, I should be back at work! Will you think about our plan, Ma?"

She nodded speechlessly.

"Julie and I will come tonight and we'll have a discussion. Now I'm going to have a word downstairs in the office and then I'll be off. You'll give me a wave as usual, eh?"

She smiled. From the time the boys were little lads setting off for school, they'd always turned to see Ailie waving goodbye from the window.

"Of course," she said affectionately. "I'll be at the window. See you tonight."

As she waited, the music from the radio seemed to swell louder. It flowed through her, quickening the beat of her heart to the sweet, long-remembered tune. She swayed, giving herself up to the music, to the feeling that David's strong arms held her in the old familiar lightness of the dance.

Nicky reached the foot of the steps and turned to look up. She waved to him, her face radiant, her smile so vivid and bright that he caught a glimpse of the Ailie Asher when she'd been a girl.

Ailie nodded back. Yes, she would be happy some day soon in her own little place beside the family. And Bay House would never be lost to her.

Always, in her mind's eye, she would see the quiet old house by the bay and, in the big sunny kitchen, two shadows dancing. □

ANDREW had hoped to spend this Christmas as he'd spen the last one. A late breakfast, steak and chips for lunch and a solitary drive to the coast.

But no.

"It's only for a couple of days, Andrew," Matt, his brother-in-law said. "You can arrive on Christmas Eve and leave on Boxing Day You'll have to come, though. Fran worries about you."

Andrew had politely declined his sister's invitation to join thei celebrations and this telephone call from Matt had caught him off guard.

"Remind her that I'm thirty-four," Andrew suggested lightly. "Ol enough to look after myself."

Matt laughed.

"I do. Constantly."

"This will be the last Christmas you spend together," Andrew said offering up a silent thank you for the sudden brainwave. "You shoul make the most of it. This time next year, you'll have the baby t think about."

Hope For

"It won't work, Andrew. That excuse isn't good enough."

Andrew groaned.

"Matt, I honestly don't feel like — "

"I know," Matt interrupted sympathetically, "but I have to take 'ran's side on this. She ruined last Christmas by worrying about you being on your own. And in her condition, I don't want her fretting."

In the face of this emotional blackmail, Andrew said the only thing ıe could. A hollow, "Thank you," followed by an untrue, "I'll look orward to it."

It wasn't that Andrew didn't like Christmas. It was simply that it vas too painful a reminder of how little he had to celebrate.

Christmas was a time for children, not adults. Andrew could still ecall his own breathless anticipation, trying to stay awake, determined to catch a glimpse of Santa Claus.

He knew the "goodwill to all men" smiles that appeared at Christmas would disappear as soon as the festivities were over.

ON Christmas Eve, Andrew drove to his sister and brother-in-law's house.

Fran had carefully attached their cards to wide strips of red ibbon. The stone mantelpiece was trimmed with fir cones, holly, and ed and green candles. Mistletoe hung in every room.

Centre stage was the enormous spruce, with its branches drooping beneath the weight of baubles, tinsel and flashing lights.

Andrew was there because he didn't want Fran to worry. In two veeks' time, Fran would present him with a niece or nephew. He ppreciated that pregnant women had to be indulged, but he couldn't ıelp thinking that Fran had never looked healthier or happier.

She'd been shopping every day for the last month and she must ıave spent hours wrapping presents, decorating the house and baking.

What was it all for, Andrew wondered. So that they could over-eat vhilst remembering white Christmases they'd known as children?

"I'm glad you're here, Andrew," Fran said warmly.

"So am I." Andrew hoped his smile didn't look too forced. 'Thanks for inviting me."

She wasn't fooled for a moment.

The Future

by SHIRLEY WORRALL

"It's not good to be alone at Christmas."

Andrew patted her hand.

"I'm fine, Fran. Honestly. I eat, I sleep — I'm coping."

Fran studied his face, noting the dark circles beneath his eyes and the hollow cheeks. She was about to comment but then changed her mind.

"We'll go to church tonight and sing carols," she said lightly.

THE church was filled to overflowing and long before the organist struck up the first notes of "Silent Night," Andrew wondered how many would be at church the following Sunday.

Cynic, he chided himself.

If only Rachel could have been by his side, he felt sure he'd see some meaning to it all. If only he could see her kneeling beside a Christmas tree they'd decorated together. If only he could kiss her laughing face beneath the mistletoe . . .

Andrew felt quite guilty as they left the church. The entire service had been lost on him. He'd been reliving other Christmases. Times when Christmas had brought joy and happiness, when it had been so much more than a couple of lonely days to endure.

Back at the house, they drank hot chocolate before Fran and Matt headed for bed.

"I'll be going up soon," Andrew told them.

"No peeking at the presents," Fran teased.

Left alone, Andrew picked up the photo frame that sat on the bookshelf. The photograph was one of his favourites.

It showed him and Rachel leaving the church in a shower of confetti. Two laughing people, very much in love and confident that the years stretched endlessly before them.

They hadn't known how little time they had, how short Rachel's life was to be.

Andrew returned the frame to its place on the bookshelf. He ate, he slept, he coped. But happiness was out of reach.

That night, he didn't sleep at all.

He heard the commotion just after half past two and crept out of bed to investigate.

"It's the baby," a panic-stricken Matt explained. "I'm taking Fran to the hospital."

"But it's not due — "

"Another two weeks." Matt nodded, his face turning a shade paler every second.

"Is there anything I can do?" Andrew asked.

Matt shook his head.

"Yes," Fran called out. "Put my bag in the car and make sure the car starts — No, better still, you can drive us to the hospital, Andrew. I'd like to get there in one piece and the state Matt's in, there's no knowing what might happen."

Andrew drove them to the hospital. He was shaking so much it was difficult to change gear. Matt looked near to collapse, he noticed.

Fran, however, was giving them a run-down on the freezer's contents and calmly telling them how to cook a turkey.

The night dragged. After leaving them at the hospital, Andrew drove back to the house. He wished he could telephone their parents, and Matt's, but Fran had told him to wait in case it was a false alarm.

He wished there was something — anything — he could do to pass the time.

Eventually, he returned to the hospital to haunt corridors which were a bright rainbow of streamers and tinsel.

When he finally saw Matt, there was no need to ask if all was well. His brother-in-law's anxious expression had been replaced by the biggest grin Andrew had ever seen.

"A boy," Matt announced, shaking his head in wonder. "Seven pounds ten ounces. A big, strong, healthy boy."

"And Fran?"

"Over the moon," Matt said, and it was clear that emotion was about to get the better of him.

LATER, Andrew went along to the nursery for his first glimpse of his nephew.

Through the glass, he saw seven babies in identical cribs. If the colours of the blankets were accurate, there were three girls and four boys.

Seeing him standing there, a nurse came out.

"A proud father?" she asked.

Andrew shook his head.

"A proud uncle. My sister — Mrs Thorp."

Smiling, the nurse pointed to one of the cribs.

"Your nephew. Noel Matthew Thorp."

"Noel?" Andrew laughed. "The last I heard it was gong to be David or Alice."

The nurse smiled and then turned to go back to the nursery.

"Merry Christmas," she said.

As Andrew watched Noel Matthew Thorp punching the air with his mitten-clad fists, his heart filled.

There was so much for this child to see. So much to do, so much to learn and so many decisions to be made. Would he make the right decisions or the wrong ones? Would his dreams come true? Just what did his life hold in store?

No-one knew, of course.

But come what may, they would all rejoice in his successes and commiserate with his failures. He was a part of their lives, their first precious link to the next generation.

This was what Christmas was all about, Andrew realised. This is what it had always been about. The birth of a child. A new beginning, bringing with it fresh hope for the future.

The blue blankets were given a sharp kick and Andrew laughed softly.

"Merry Christmas!" he whispered. "And thank you . . ." □

MORNING, Mrs Walker. Surprise for you this morning." The postman smiled, handing Hilary a parcel.

She pulled a wry face.

"I'm afraid it's just something for my husband. No, Carol!" She thwarted her ten-month-old daughter's attempts to climb the postman's legs.

She swung Carol into her arms, and the postman grinned.

"Into everything at that age, aren't they?"

Stretching out her chubby arms, Carol leaned forward.

"Mamma, Mamma," she crowed.

The postman chuckled.

"Well, I've been called some things in my time, but that beats the band!"

"It's the only word she can say," her mother explained. "But even I'm getting sick of the sound of it."

"She's stupid!" David, aged nine, spoke from behind Hilary.

"Nose out of joint, is it?" the postman said. "I remember one of mine was like that. But he got over it. They all do."

Hilary just hoped he might be right.

Back in the kitchen, she fastened the baby in her high-chair, and went back to washing the breakfast dishes.

David stood in the middle of the room, watching her. As Carol threw the last of her toys to the floor, he made a face.

"She's stupid," he said again.

Hilary turned round and began to pick up the toys, returning them to the tray in front of the baby.

"Don't use that word about your sister, David. Carol's a baby. She doesn't know all the things you know."

"That's for sure!" David was out to annoy her. "Calling the postman Mamma. I ask you!"

"She wasn't. She doesn't know what the word means

"Where Did I Go Wrong?"

by
PHYLLIS
HEATH

yet. She's too little."

David never called her "Mother", or anything else, come to that.

"It's just a sound, like when she used to gurgle. All babies say it," Hilary explained. "In a little while she'll begin to understand it means me."

"Because you are *her* mother," David said with studied insolence.

"Because I'm the person who looks after her, takes care of her, loves her. That's what 'Mother' means," Hilary said quietly.

David stopped glaring. He seemed to be considering her words, and she held her breath. But then his face closed.

"Can I go and play in the garden now?"

She let him go. There was no way she could make David love her. She had to be grateful that he at least tolerated her presence here, in the house he had shared with his real mother.

David and Brian had lived here for two years after Lucy died, before Hilary had even met them. Brian Walker worked for the same firm, and she'd heard of his tragic loss, but until Hilary gained promotion they'd seldom come into contact.

By that time, the bleak look had left Brian's eyes and he had learned to laugh again, to tease the girls in the office — and to notice them.

Brian found himself liking the quiet way Hilary worked, her air of assurance, her friendly warmth. He gravitated to her table in the canteen, her desk at coffee breaks, and it became habit to walk to the car park together.

From the start Hilary knew she was falling in love with him, but she imagined that on his part it was just friendship. She didn't want to spoil that, so she tried to hide her own feelings. But she stopped going out with anyone else.

Ironically, it was David who turned the scales in her favour. He caught measles, and Brian was quite worried. He talked to her about it, and she bought small gifts for David to while away his convalescence.

By way of thanks, once David was fit again, Brian took her to dinner at a smart place in town, where they could talk.

Driving home, Brian stopped in a quiet lane, and kissed her.

"I think I'm in love with you," he told her, his voice full of amazement. "I didn't think I could ever feel this way about anyone again.

"Though I'll never forget Lucy —"

Hilary put a finger across his lips.

"I understand," she whispered. "I love you, Brian, and I'll settle for half your love."

It wasn't like that, though. Soon Brian found it was possible to love Hilary just as much as he had Lucy — but in a different way.

THEY were married in the spring, when David was almost eight. Hilary gave her stepson his first birthday party since Lucy had died. It was her first attempt to get close to the small boy.

Brian hadn't envisaged any problems.

"He was so young when Lucy died — he couldn't understand. But he'll love you, I know he will. Who could help loving you?"

She wanted to love his son, wanted David to come to love her, but as the weeks grew into months she began to despair.

"He's too quiet, Brian. Was he always this way?"

Brian shook his head.

"Not with Lucy, but since then . . . He'll get over it, you'll see. Now we're a family again he'll be able to have his friends round, like other kids. With me out at work, things were awkward."

Obviously David enjoyed having more time with his friends and having his father around, but he treated Hilary with a wary acceptance which worried her.

Had he been told stories in which wicked stepmothers played a part? Brian laughed at her fears.

"He's been too old for fairytales for a long time. I'm sure you're worrying needlessly. He seems fine to me."

"Brian, I don't think we live with the same child," Hilary said in exasperation. Didn't he see the boy who answered her in monosyllables, and said please and thank you, like a polite guest?

When she found she was pregnant, her main concern was how David would take the news.

"We must tell him quite soon, before he hears it from outsiders," she urged.

Brian, thrilled about the coming baby, agreed.

"Perhaps this will do the trick," he said.

So he had been worrying after all!

"I thought you said there was nothing wrong," Hilary accused.

"Well, I thought it would pass, but it's been almost a year. I can't make him out. He seems normal otherwise, getting into mischief with the others."

They were lying close together in the darkness of their room.

"I've done all I can," she told him. "I just don't seem to get through to him."

"Perhaps you're trying too hard. I mean, when the baby comes and it's a bit bigger, you won't *try* to love it, will you? You won't have to, not like with David."

Hilary felt herself go cold.

Already she loved the coming baby, and she wanted to love David, too.

Perhaps that's what's wrong, she thought. Does he sense that whatever I say, or do, I don't really love him?

She began to try harder to show her feelings, ruffling the small boy's hair, hugging him warmly on his return from school, biting her tongue when she might have spoken sharply to him.

When they told him about the coming baby, David received the news with a nonchalance beyond his years.

"What will it be? I hope it's a boy. Girls are soppy."

Hilary held her peace. They knew they were to have a girl, and were both pleased, but there was no point in telling David.

"He'll have got used to having her around long before her sex makes any difference," Brian said. "Anyway, I remember wishing I had a sister to take care of when I was his age. Us men like to feel protective!"

Hilary kissed him. Boys could also be stubborn; she had two brothers of her own.

Brian brought David to the hospital once the baby arrived.

"She's awful small," he complained.

Brian laughed.

"You weren't much bigger yourself. She'll grow."

"But she's a girl! Girls don't play football."

"Some do. With a brother like you, Carol might even play rugby."

David shot him a scornful look, but he did take a little interest in his sister once she got home, watching as Hilary bathed and fed her, touching her tentatively.

"She's real," he said. "She's got nails on her fingers, and eyelashes — well, a few — and she looks at me."

Hilary didn't tell him the baby couldn't see him properly yet. She offered to let him hold the baby, but he backed away.

"I don't think I like babies much," he mumbled.

Brian and Hilary exchanged a smile over the boy's head. Despite what he said, David was hooked.

That night, Hilary lay cuddled into the curve of Brian's arm.

"I think it's going to be all right," she murmured. "But we've got to be careful he doesn't get jealous. Carol takes up so much time and attention . . . I wouldn't want him to think I don't want him now. And you must be extra careful, Brian."

NOW, months later, she knew that their troubles had just been beginning. The quiet, polite child was now a noisy, rude monster.

David seemed to take a perverse pleasure in tormenting the baby, running past where she sat on the rug so that her eyes followed him, and she overbalanced. Moving her toys up out of reach when she learned to crawl . . .

It's only a phase, Hilary told herself. It'll pass. But it didn't.

Brian, true to his word, spent a lot of time with David, taking him to places which weren't possible with a baby in tow.

"We've tried so hard not to let him feel he's taken second place. How can he still be jealous?" Hilary asked Brian.

As Carol became more mobile, Hilary found her nerves stretched to breaking point. Twice she only just saved treasured ornaments supposedly out of Carol's reach.

David was becoming more unruly. "Why should I?" was constantly on his lips.

"He stands there and defies me, and there's something about the way he looks at me," she told Brian. "I'd swear he was almost smiling, in a strange kind of way. Taunting me. As if he knows I won't really punish him."

"Darling, I'm sorry. I never dreamed it would be like this." Brian sighed, and Hilary's heart contracted. Hadn't her husband suffered

STAITHES, NORTH YORKSHIRE

ACCORDING to the dictionary, a staith is a waterside coal depot equipped for loading vessels, and certainly in years gone by, smugglers did a great deal of loading and unloading in this village clinging to the Yorkshire coast. But Staithes has also won its place in history as a centre for artists, with the Staithes Group, of which Dame Laura Knight was a member, flourishing around the turn of the century.

STAITHES, YORKSHIRE : J CAMPBELL KERR

enough heartbreak in the past?

"I'm just scared of making him hate me even more," she confessed.

"He doesn't hate you!" Brian protested.

"Maybe not, but I've taken his mother's place, and he does resent that."

Brian held her close as she began to cry.

"I'm sorry, darling," he whispered.

Next day Hilary felt far from well, and the fact that it was a school holiday didn't help. However, David played quite happily in the garden with his friends. It was Carol who seemed bent on mischief.

Whenever Hilary turned her back, her daughter was off, pushing her teddy into the washing-machine, emptying the salad drawer, taking the pans off the rack, every bit of mischief her active brain could dream up.

Each time, Hilary spoke sternly, tapping her daughter's hand, but Carol simply looked at her with large, solemn eyes. In seconds, she was into mischief again.

In the end, fear made Hilary lose her temper. Running back from the bathroom, she was just in time to snatch the child from her precarious perch on the step-stool.

Scarcely aware of what she was doing, she brought her open palm down on her daughter's legs.

The small body froze for a second, then an ear-splitting roar rent the air.

Hilary was astounded by what she'd done. As the screams turned to sobs, she sat on the stool, the child cuddled in her arms, her body shaking.

"I'm sorry, darling. You were very naughty," she whispered. "You really were."

YOU smacked her!" David's horrified voice brought Hilary spinning round. "Carol's crying 'cause you smacked her!"

"She was very naughty, David. She might have been badly hurt. I was very scared."

"But don't you love her any more?"

"David!" Instinctively, Hilary tightened her arms round the baby, smoothing her cheeks and kissing her gently. "What a thing to say. Of course I haven't stopped loving her.

"I shouldn't have smacked her, but I was scared."

"But you've never smacked her before. Even when she cried at bedtime."

"No, that was different. She's got to learn, David. I can't always be watching her. She's got to learn not to do dangerous things.

"It's because I love her that I must get her to obey me. She can't grow up doing just what she wants." Hilary laughed, a little uncertainly, still shaken by the force of her fear.

David watched her as she rocked her daughter.

"She's gone to sleep," he said after a moment. "It mustn't hurt any more."

My Shadow

AS I walk home to have my tea,
My shadow walks along with me.
When I skip, then he skips, too.
He copies everything I do.

I clap my hands and his hands meet,
And just like me he's got two feet.
I nod, he nods. It's such fun
Playing with him in the sun.

As I walk home to have my tea,
The sun grows pale and so does he.
And when the sun has gone from view,
I know that he will vanish, too.

— Helen Russell.

Hilary stood up. "No, I don't think it really hurt. She got a shock, that's all. Poor little pet," she whispered. "Mummy didn't mean to hurt you."

She carried Carol to her cot, standing a moment to look down at the sleeping child. As she turned away, she heard a crash from downstairs, followed by a strange silence.

David was standing in the kitchen when she hurried down. He was facing her, his head high, the remains of her largest mixing bowl at his feet.

There was no way he could have broken the bowl accidentally. Hilary stared at the pieces, then at David, and she began to understand.

Deliberately, she stepped across the mess and smacked his legs.

She saw the tears begin, and reached out to hug him close.

Once the tears were over, and he lay against her, his head beneath her chin, he started to talk at last.

"My other mummy smacked me when I was very naughty." He raised his head, and mischief gleamed in his eyes; mischief, and something else.

"But I was never as naughty as this," he said with satisfaction.

"And you'd better never be again, my lad. Oh, David, David! What a great silly I've been."

She laughed, holding him close once more.

It wasn't over, she knew. There would be other stormy times, but they'd made a start.

When Brian got home that evening, he was stunned by his wife's radiant smile.

"It seems I'm a proper mum now," she said. □

Rainbow's End

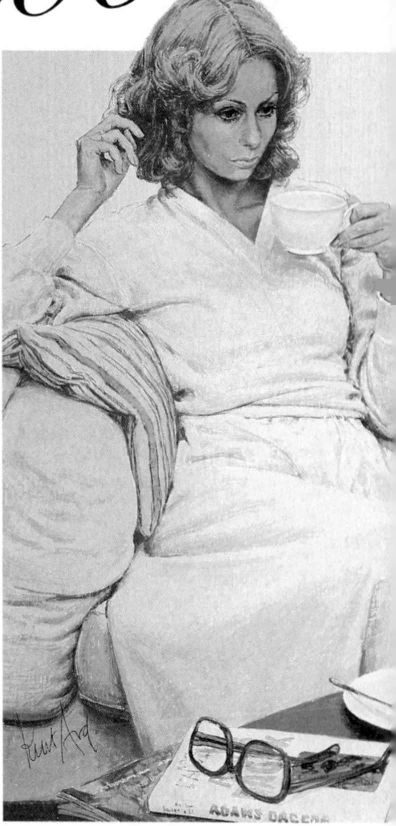

"I REALLY wanted something a shade darker."

The customer looked consideringly at the bolt of satin Grace Mackenzie was showing her.

"Haven't you a peach? Or even a soft yellow?"

"I'm sorry." Grace shook her head.

In all her years at Reid's Fabrics and Soft Furnishings, she'd prided herself upon keeping her department well stocked. It embarrassed her to see the polished wooden shelves practically bare.

During recent weeks, there'd been no deliveries of new stock. Grace had been forced to turn away almost as many customers as she'd actually sold goods to.

Watching the woman leave empty-handed, Grace sighed in exasperation. At the end of the day, Grace locked up her till and took the meagre takings up to Murdo Reid's office.

Despite the rumours circulating amongst the staff, and the shop's run-down appearance, Murdo Reid had nothing to say to his employees. It wasn't fair, Grace decided as she left by the side door.

If Reid's *was* going to close down, why couldn't Murdo tell them — and put an end to the agonising wondering and waiting?

Grace lived in a top-floor flat not five minutes' walk from the shop. What a godsend that had been when Mother's health was failing. She'd been able to pop home at lunchtime, and towards the end, even during her tea breaks.

Grace hurried homewards, past the rows of shops. She paused, yet again, at the window of the second-hand shop. Yes, it was still there.

by KJELL DAVIES

Grace felt the cold drizzle against her cheeks. Amateur though it was, that little painting had a quality that pleased her.

It showed a Highland scene, capturing the slowly changing colours of hill, loch and glen as rain turned to sunshine and a vivid rainbow arched across the brightening sky.

Grace made up her mind. She strode into the shop, emerging a few moments later with the water-colour tucked under her arm.

GRACE'S older brother, Donald, was an insurance agent in Galashiels. Once a month, he came into Glasgow, to head office, and called in at Grace's flat before returning home.

"That's new," Donald remarked, pointing his pipe towards the water-colour, which Grace had framed and stood on the mantelpiece.

"Don't you like it?"

"It's all right." He considered "Somewhere up north, isn't it?"

"Looks a glorious place for a holiday," Grace replied. "And I may well get a much longer holiday than usual this year!" she added wryly.

"Reid's, you mean? From what you say, closure seems to be on the cards right enough."

They chatted until Donald had finished his pipe and then he got up to leave.

"I've finished crocheting a shawl for Susie's new baby."

Grace fetched the whisper-light cockleshell pink shawl.

"I had intended posting it, but perhaps you could give it to her when you next see her?"

"Of course. Madge and I'll be going at the weekend. This is very nice." Donald held up the shawl, admiring Grace's beautiful handiwork.

It stirred an old memory, one that made him uneasy. Grace had once come to him with the burning ambition to open her own shop. She wanted to sell wool and thread and suchlike, and her own hand-made garments.

"Donald?" Grace prompted. "You look very solemn all of a sudden!"

"Just thinking back. I do it more and more these days." He folded the baby's shawl carefully.

"You always were a fine needlewoman, Grace. And you've a sensible head on your shoulders. I reckon you'd have made a success of that wee shop you wanted."

"Goodness, I hadn't thought of that in years!" Grace laughed, helping him on with his heavy overcoat. "Dad nearly had a fit when I put the idea to him."

"He was set in his ways, but we might have talked him round," Donald admitted uncomfortably. "I should've backed you up."

"You had a career of your own to worry about — and a young family," she replied simply. "Besides, after Dad died, Mother couldn't have managed alone."

IT was scarcely a surprise when Murdo Reid called his employees into his office. But it still shocked Grace when he told them the shop was closing down.

She suddenly realised how important work was to her. Over the years, she'd built her whole life around Reid's. And now it was gone . . .

At first, Grace was more alarmed and afraid than she admitted even to herself. However, by the time Donald came for his usual monthly visit, she'd begun making plans.

"You're off on holiday?" Donald exclaimed as she took his hat and scarf.

"Away to the Highlands!" Grace replied enthusiastically. "Just like in my water-colour!" she added with a chuckle.

"Everything's arranged. I'm taking a round trip. I've booked into a hotel in Duirloch, where I'm staying until Easter. Then I'm touring.

"Inverness, the Cairngorms, Loch Lomond, Castle Rock . . ." Grace's pale, slim features were bright and animated. "Oh, I want to see it all!"

"That sounds like a lot of travelling," Donald commented, filling his pipe. "Are you going by coach?"

"Oh no, I intend getting myself a wee car," Grace told him.

"It might be wiser to wait a while before going on holiday — and buying a car," Donald advised, drawing on his pipe. "Finding a new job might be much harder than you expect. Work is hard to come by these days."

"You're quite right, of course," Grace conceded seriously. "But I'm not badly off. I've my nest-egg of savings, and my redundancy money from Reid's.

"I don't expect you'll understand, Donald, but this holiday is terribly important to me.

"I feel as though I've never achieved anything in my life," she went on earnestly. "Never *done* anything.

"Getting in a car, leaving the city and just driving away out into the countryside is something I've often dreamed about.

"Now I've the chance to make my dream come true. I must do it, Donald. I really must!"

A BLUSTERY March wind blew Grace and her wee second-hand car into the Highland village of Duirloch.

After asking directions from the postmaster, she continued on towards The Bell Inn, a mile or so beyond the village.

Coming over the top of the hill, Grace gasped in delight at the shimmering expanse of clear, blue water sparkling away into the distance below her.

The banks of the loch were fringed with evergreens and stands of old trees. Here and there, weathered cottages dotted the banks, with a handful reaching up into soft, green hills, beyond which rose hazy, purple mountains.

The Bell was an early eighteenth-century inn built from stone at the lochside, where the bank curved so sharply it almost doubled back upon itself.

After the long journey from Glasgow, Grace gratefully stretched her legs and breathed in the cool, crisp air as she started along the steep path up to the inn.

"I'm Jenny Carmichael," a girl of about twenty with a neat bob of curly hair greeted her cheerfully.

"Dad usually likes to welcome our guests himself, but he's away on the hill with a party of birdwatchers."

Jenny showed Grace up a broad staircase and swung open a door. The room had a high, dark-beamed ceiling and three square wee windows set into the thick, creamy-washed stone walls.

"The Bell is open all year round, but we don't get really busy until after Easter. Apart from the birdwatchers, you've got the inn all to yourself." Jenny smiled.

"It's an interesting old place. Feel free to wander around. If you need anything, just let me know . . ."

Grace liked the homely atmosphere of The Bell, and quickly settled in. She discovered some lovely walks through wooded glens where the first flowers of spring were showing their colours, and joined the birdwatchers on long, exhilarating hikes.

The evenings were spent quietly at The Bell's fireside sewing or reading, or simply listening to Jenny play the piano.

Sometimes she'd accompany her father's singing. Alastair not only had a fine tenor voice, but was a soloist with Duirloch's church choir.

She could hear Alastair singing as she came down one damp morning when the mist was clinging above the loch.

Grace had decided against joining Jenny and the birdwatchers on a crack-of-dawn outing. Instead she planned to go down into the busy village, which she still hadn't fully explored.

"What would you like for breakfast, Miss Mackenzie?" Alastair Carmichael popped his head into the dining-room, where Grace sat alone.

"With Jenny out, and our Mrs McVitie not due in until lunchtime," he went on with a broad smile, "I'm in charge. So what'll it be?"

"Just tea and toast, please."

"Coming up —" Alastair frowned, surveying the dining-room.

"This room's a bit bleak in the morning. It doesn't get any sun, even when there's sunshine to be got. If you wouldn't mind eating with me in the kitchen? It *is* a bit cheerier . . ."

The warm, stone-flagged kitchen was indeed much brighter, and Alastair chatted away as he prepared breakfast.

Grace was surprised to hear that the Carmichaels had lived at The Bell for only four years.

"We're originally from Aberdeen. I was in computer analysis. It was a very competitive field. Aggressive. Demanding. I'm ashamed to admit that I thrived on it."

But Grace noticed a shadow darkening his eyes.

"After I lost my wife, it was all too easy for me to immerse myself completely in my career. Then a heart attack stopped me cold.

"I was lucky. I got a second chance. And for Jenny's sake even more than my own, I *had* to re-think my lifestyle.

"We came up to the Highlands on a touring holiday, exactly as you've done. We both loved Duirloch and The Bell was for sale . . ."

Alastair smiled down at her now, his eyes twinkling. "And here we are!"

SOON Grace came to know Duirloch fairly well.

The week before Easter she and Jenny were in the village together shopping, and they took an unfamiliar short cut towards the newsagent's. As soon as Grace saw the narrow wee corner house, she was instantly taken back to her childhood.

The solid front door opened directly on to the pavement. The single downstairs front window was low and splayed.

"It's been empty for ages," Jenny commented. "The postman told me it was the police house, back in the olden days when the village had its own bobby!" She laughed. "It certainly doesn't *look* much like a police station, does it!"

"No, it doesn't," Grace replied absently. "It looks exactly like the wee corner shop I knew as a girl in Glasgow. They were just ordinary houses, but the front room had been turned into a tiny shop that sold everything from candied peel to kettles."

She gazed up at the corner house wistfully, unaware that Jenny was watching her.

"The keys are at the post office," the girl began impulsively. "I've always wanted to see inside this house, but it wouldn't have been any fun on my own. Let's get the keys and take a look!"

The square front room had been the village constable's office. It still had shelving and pigeon-holes around two walls, and the high, mahogany counter across its width.

Grace allowed her fancy to fly. At once she imagined the room as her wee wool shop, every corner crammed with knitting yarns,

HIDDEN VILLAGES OF SCOTLAND

CARRADALE

HALFWAY down the forty-mile-long peninsula extending southwards from Crinan to the Mull of Kintyre lies the charming village of Carradale. It's a sweet little place with a natural rock-girt harbour that is always colourful with inshore fishing boats and pleasure craft — not forgetting the colourful folk who man them!

The main road to Campbeltown and the Mull keeps to the western fringe of Kintyre, but the road to Carradale (on the east side) is the more adventurous. Here are rocky hillocks and ferny dells, lochans studded with white waterlilies or all a-wave with cotton grass, hump-backed bridges and hairpin bends. Obviously it's a road never intended for fast driving, but who would want to, with so much to see?

There are hedgerows of fuchsia, thickets of gorse, and every now and then a glimpse of Arran, only three miles distant across Kilbrennan Sound. In sunshine, after a shower of rain, it looks even nearer, and you can see the gleam of white-harled cottages along the shoreline.

Notice Aird Castle, quite near Carradale's miniature pier. It's a ruin now, but in its heyday it was proudly linked with the Lords of the Isles, and even King Robert the Bruce himself.

buttons, ribbons, trimmings, lace, needles, baby linen and hand-mades.

She found herself enthusiastically sharing her thoughts with Jenny Carmichael. The whole story came spilling out as they wandered through to the rear room with its ancient, black-leaded grate.

"You're really keen on this place, aren't you?" Jenny said excitedly. "It's just perfect for your shop!"

Reality brought Grace down to earth with an abrupt bump.

"It would've been. Years ago. When I was your age. But now . . . Oh, I was just thinking aloud. Daydreaming!"

"There's nothing wrong with dreaming," Jenny replied firmly. "Without our dreams, we'd never accomplish anything!"

"I agree." Grace smiled, as she turned the key and locked the front door. "But some dreams can be won, others you have to let go of . . ."

THE crisp Highland air and her long country walks, combined with The Bell's hearty home-cooking, had put roses into Grace's cheeks and filled out her spare figure with flattering curves.

She was sewing at the fireside, adjusting the waistband of her pleated skirt, and listening to Jenny play for Alastair to rehearse for the Easter Day services.

"Dad — I really have to go and help Mrs McVitie in the kitchen." Jenny lifted her fingers from the well-worn keys.

"Can't we go through it at least once more?" Alastair protested. "I want to be perfect!"

Jenny glanced around to where Grace was slipping her needle back into its case.

"Grace — do you play the piano?"

"Can't you see Grace is busy?" Alastair murmured.

"I'm finished, really. And I'd be happy to play," Grace replied with a smile. "I'm just not sure I still remember how . . ."

"I really appreciate your help," Alastair said a while later, when he was as satisfied with his preparations as he was ever likely to be. "I'm sorry Jenny press-ganged you into playing. She doesn't mean to be pushy, it's just her way."

"Jenny's exuberant, nothing wrong with that! And besides, I thoroughly enjoyed it." Grace's fingers moved lightly over the keys as she spoke. "I'd almost forgotten how much I loved to play."

"That's beautiful," Alastair remarked, sitting down beside her. " 'Clair de lune', isn't it?"

"So it is! I hadn't even realised I was playing it. I saw a film once, which began with it. I've loved it ever since."

"Me too. I've never forgotten the music, but I'm blowed if I recall a thing about the film!" Alastair laughed, then hesitated.

"Grace, there's a touring production of 'Swan Lake' performing over at Aultmoor on Saturday evening. Would you like to go?"

★ ★ ★ ★

Grace had never enjoyed an evening more than that Easter Saturday.

However, the wonderful dancing and the haunting beauty of Tchaikovsky's music and the pleasure she found in Alastair Carmichael's companionship were clouded. Saturday was also the end of Grace's stay at The Bell.

Tomorrow she would leave for Inverness.

IT was still dark when Grace awoke on Easter Day.

Gusts of rain swirled across the loch to batter against the windowpanes as she moved about her room collecting her belongings and packing her cases. She'd set off straight after church.

Tiptoeing down to the kitchen for a cup of tea, Grace stifled a cry of alarm, swiftly followed by an incredulous chuckle. She had collided in the near-darkness of the hallway with Alastair, clad in a voluminous yellow mackintosh and sou'wester, and carrying a bulging plastic carrier bag.

"What on earth —?"

"Going out into the garden to hide the Easter eggs," Alastair whispered tersely. "The children will be coming to search for them after church."

"The rain may have cleared by then," Grace reasoned. "Can't you hide the eggs later?"

"Daren't leave it until daylight," Alastair replied grimly. "Inquisitive little eyes have a habit of peeping. . ."

He unlocked the garden door as Grace sped upstairs.

"Wait for me!" she called quietly over the banister. "I'll just get my mac."

After church, when Grace was ready to leave, Jenny Carmichael hugged her warmly.

"I do wish you could stay. You're part of the family now!"

Grace returned the girl's hug and blinked back a tear, She knew Jenny's words were sincere.

"Here come the Easter egg hunters!" Jenny giggled as the first of the children bounded up the path towards the inn. "I must go. Drive safely, Grace!"

"Inverness is a long drive," Alastair commented mechanically, walking with Grace to her car. "At least the weather's improved."

"Yes. It's very pleasant."

The children's excited voices rang out from the wooded gardens beyond The Bell, and a great cheer went up as the first Easter egg was found.

"We must keep in touch, Grace," Alastair said suddenly. "Perhaps you could visit us again. Or maybe I . . . we . . . will come down to Glasgow.

"After all," he concluded, his voice deliberately light, "it's not as though Duirloch and Glasgow are a world apart, is it?"

Oh, but they are, Grace thought pensively. They are!

Glasgow was where she belonged. Her flat, her whole life was there. And when she got settled into a new job . . . Well, she'd probably never return to Duirloch.

For the next few hours, Grace kept her eyes fixed upon the road stretching before her.

But however fiercely she tried, she couldn't blot out the pictures and memories that flooded her mind.

The village . . . The old inn at the lochside . . . Sunny-natured Jenny . . . That wee corner house, standing empty and waiting.

Grace swallowed hard, not wishing to recall the sadness in Alastair Carmichael's eyes when they'd parted, not wanting to remember the many lovely hours they'd shared . . .

Purple shadows of twilight were stealing down from the hills when Grace returned to Duirloch.

Her spirit soared when she saw Alastair Carmichael standing alone on the lochside, watching the colours of sunset fading into the clear water.

"I was going to follow you," he murmured at last, when Grace stood at his side. "And ask you to come back."

Grace nodded silently, and Alastair offered her his hand. Together, they started towards the beckoning lights of the inn. □

IT'S too bad you have to go to the office today," Emma Nicholls moaned, as her husband pulled on his jacket.

She spread the newspaper she'd gone out to buy on the kitchen table.

Robert hugged her.

"I'm sorry, sweetheart. Every fourth Saturday — it's part of the job."

"Oh, I know, but I could have done with your help today. There's so much to do for the party . . ."

"I'm sure you'll have everything under control, love — you always do."

"What time will you be home?"

"About half-past five, I should think." He paused. "I can give you a hand then, so don't go exhausting yourself.

"At least we'll both be able to take it easy at Mum's tomorrow. 'Bye for now, love."

Emma's smile felt brittle as she waved goodbye. He knew perfectly well that she found it hard to relax at her mother-in-law's house.

It wasn't that they didn't get on. She just couldn't understand how Celia seemed content to live in a perpetual muddle. Surrounded by the clutter of a dozen different needlework projects and half a dozen cats, Celia cheerfully ignored the conventions of regular meals — and washing-up, for that matter!

Emma went back into the kitchen to have a quick glance at the paper, then wash the breakfast things. She wanted to start on the salmon mousse as soon as possible, so that it would have time to set.

She worked calmly and methodically, laying out all the necessary ingredients and utensils, and leaning the cookery book against the toaster.

This meal *had* to be perfect. She wanted to create a right impression for Robert's boss and his wife. Besides, David and Jacqui had given them such a lovely meal a few weeks ago . . .

A LITTLE GIVE

Following the recipe closely, Emma was just mixing the ingredients when the doorbell rang.

She groaned inwardly. "I'm busy — go away," she muttered as she hurried down the passage. But as she opened the door she forced a bright smile.

Her mother-in-law smiled back equally brightly, but with more warmth. Bending down, she pulled a bundle of newspaper-wrapped flowers from the top of her bulging basket.

"Hello, dear. I knew I'd be passing, so I thought I'd drop in. The garden's lovely at the moment; so many daffodils that it would be a sin not to share them."

AND TAKE

by
KAREN
McAULAY

She paused, holding a hand to her heaving chest.
"Phew! It's windy out today — I'm quite puffed."
"Thank$, Mum. What a kind thought. Look — come on in and get 'our breath back. I was about to put the kettle on."
The older woman followed her in gratefully, and sank on to a :itchen chair. Seeing the mixing-bowls, she peered forward to look at he recipe book.
"That looks ambitious."
Emma turned to fill the kettle.
"Robert's boss and his wife are coming over tonight."
"I haven't interrupted you at a crucial stage, have I?"

"No, not really," Emma lied. "I'll just put it into the mould while the kettle's boiling."

"You go ahead," Celia said easily. "What else are they having?"

"Boeuf en croûte," Emma pronounced carefully. "Then lemon meringue or apricot cheesecake. Then a cheese-board."

"Sooner you than me! Still, you look well organised."

"I do my best." It's how I was brought up, Emma thought privately.

"Still, I expect you'll be ready for a wee break, if you've been working all morning." Celia nodded understandingly.

"Mmm — just a little one," Emma agreed, not having the heart to admit she was working to a tight schedule.

FORCING herself to sit and drink her coffee companionably, Emma listened patiently as Celia chattered away. How on earth was she going to get back to work without appearing rude?

She'd almost made up her mind to start on the desserts, when Celia took her last sip of coffee. Standing up, she put her cup on the draining-board.

"Well, dear, I'd better let you get on. I'll see you tomorrow. Any time. Just come whenever it suits you."

"'Bye, Mum. Thanks again for the flowers!"

Emma closed the door with a sigh of relief. She had jotted down a list of things that had to be done, and now she consulted it thoughtfully. Good, she wasn't too far behind.

Clearing up after the mousse, Emma washed the dishes, and flicked through a different cookery book to find her cheesecake recipe.

At three o'clock, she paused for breath and wiped her forehead wearily. The meal was well under way. She had a full fridge to prove it.

What next?

Deciding to leave the beef until later, she pulled out her dusters and the vacuum cleaner, and set to work in the living-room. Even if she didn't clean upstairs, she wanted to give downstairs a thorough going-over.

She sighed. The dinner-party tonight, then Sunday with Celia. What a weekend! Going to work would seem like a rest by comparison . . .

Suddenly ashamed of herself, she polished the coffee-table particularly vigorously as a penance. Not a speck of dust would dare to show itself by the time she'd finished!

By the time Robert was due home, Emma was feeling a quiet glow of satisfaction. Apart from putting the beef into the oven at the appropriate time, there was really nothing much left to do.

She opened the dining-room door to gaze at the shining wine glasses and lovingly-polished candlesticks. Not a bad day's work, she murmured contentedly.

A glance in the hall mirror confirmed that her hair had obligingly stayed tidy, too. She hoped Robert would be proud of her.

The minutes ticked by. She went across to the window and looked down the street. There was no sign of him.

A quarter, then another half an hour passed . . . Feeling rather foolish, Emma dialled Robert's office number. A recorded message politely informed her that there was no-one there to take her call.

She put the phone down angrily. Her mind was seething with alarming possibilities.

Had the car broken down? Or been stolen? Or involved in an accident? How long should she wait before ringing the police?

The sound of the doorbell was so unexpected that she started violently. David and Jacqui weren't due yet — were they?

"Hello, Emma — we're not too early, are we?" Jacqui asked, taking in the anxious look on Emma's face.

"I — well — not at all," Emma assured them, trying to look less harassed than she actually felt.

"Come on in. Let me take your coats. I'm afraid Robert isn't home yet. I hope he'll be back soon."

"Well, the traffic was bad this afternoon," David commented. "Robert went over to the Netherkirk site after lunch. He was going to come straight home."

"Well, let me get you both a drink," Emma suggested. "We'll give him half an hour, then — well, let's give him half an hour."

As she handed the drinks round, she smiled nervously.

"What a start to the evening, eh?"

"Don't apologise — we quite understand," Jacqui assured her. "Anyway, I can tell you've been busy today. Something smells delicious!"

"Let's hope so." Emma laughed. "It was a new re — "

The telephone interrupted her.

"Excuse me a minute," she gasped, and dashed out into the hall.

HELLO?"

"Emma — it's Robert. Listen, I'm all right, but I'm in Casualty at Netherkirk Hospital."

"There's been an accident? Oh, Robert are . . . !"

"I was lucky. I managed to walk away from it. I've just got cuts and bruises, but the police insisted I have a check-up."

"What happened?"

"I don't know." He sounded weary. "The car went out of control. It spun round and hit a tree — I think it's a write-off, Emma."

"Be honest with me — are you badly hurt?"

"No — it's nothing much. All the same, you'd better try to put David and Jacqui off. I don't think I'll be home in time for dinner."

"Too late — they're here!"

"Never! I'm sure I said seven o'clock!"

"Don't worry about it. Do you think you'll be allowed home tonight?"

"I couldn't say."

Parking Problem

WHERE have the cottage gardens gone
That once were Britain's pride?
Night scented stocks, and hollyhocks,
And lupins side by side.
Whyfore these dreary concrete slabs
Upon such precious space?
Alas, my dear, the family car
Now has the pride of place!

— Gaye Wilson.

Emma thought fast. "Then I'll ask David and Jacqui to drive me over to the hospital. We'll take it from there, OK?"

"OK. See you soon. Oh, and apologise to the others."

She took a deep breath, then exhaled slowly. Keep calm, she told herself. He says he's OK. The car doesn't matter so long as Robert's all right.

She pushed the door open, holding on to it for support as she looked anxiously from Jacqui to David.

Jacqui stood up and went across to her. Putting an arm round her shoulders, she hugged her understandingly.

"We couldn't help overhearing, Emma. Is Robert badly hurt?"

"He — he says it's nothing serious." Emma gulped, trying not to cry.

"But he doesn't know if he'll be home until the morning. I feel dreadful about this — the meal and everything — but do you think you could take me over to Netherkirk?"

"Of course, no problem." David stood up, reaching in his pocket for his keys.

"I'll just get the coats." Emma hurried into the hall.

"Don't forget your handbag," Jacqui reminded her, then hesitated slightly.

"Do you think you should take Robert's pyjamas and toilet things? Just in case?"

"Yes, good idea." Emma shivered.

"Actually, if there's a chance he might have to stay overnight . . . We were meant to be going to his mother's tomorrow morning. I'd better phone her."

She dialled Celia's number, taking another deep breath before she spoke.

"Mum — it's Emma. Robert's just phoned me. He's had an accident in the car. He says he's not too bad — but he's having a check-up at Netherkirk General. I just thought you should know . . . "

"Oh, poor lad. What's he done to himself?"

"Well, he said just a few cuts and bruises, but I think he's probably suffering from shock, too."

"Do you need a lift to the hospital?"

"It's all right, thanks. David and Jacqui are taking me. Shall I ring you from the hospital to let you know how he is?"

"No — I'll meet you there." Celia was decisive. "Give you both a bit of moral support, eh?"

"Bless you, Mum."

CELIA came over to meet them as they arrived at the hospital car-park. Dressed in her flamboyant, flowered skirt and an oversized, baggy jumper, she looked distinctly Bohemian.

As she introduced them, Emma wondered what Jacqui and David would be thinking.

"Pleased to meet you both." Celia smiled warmly, then turned to Emma, holding her arms out.

"Oh, Emma — cheer up, love. From what you said, things could have been a lot worse. Come on. Let's go and see the invalid."

Robert was lying in bed in a side ward. He had a large plaster on his nose, a fast-developing black eye and bandages on both hands. He grinned weakly.

"Hi, there. I didn't expect so many visitors!"

"Robert — does it hurt a lot?" Emma stared at him in dismay. "Your poor hands look . . ."

"It's just cuts and bruises — nothing broken. They're keeping me in overnight. I think they're worried about concussion. I should be allowed home tomorrow."

"Well, don't feel you have to hurry back to work," David assured him. "Take a few days off. Or longer, if the doctor recommends it."

"That's right — have a good rest, Robert." Jacqui nodded. "It won't hurt my husband to work a bit harder for a change!

"Come on, David. We shouldn't stay too long. Robert's looking awfully tired."

"Don't think I'm ungrateful — " Robert nodded wearily " — but I can't seem to keep my eyes open . . . "

Jacqui and David hung back tactfully as Celia gingerly kissed the less-bruised side of his face. Then Emma said goodbye, too, and they all tip-toed out.

Celia gave Emma a sympathetic squeeze, pulling her to one side to let the others go first.

"Oh, Emma, don't worry. He'll soon be on the mend," she murmured. "But — forgive me for interfering — what about your dinner? Are you planning on going back home now?"

"Heavens! The beef — it's still in the oven! I'll have to go back. Er — excuse me a minute . . ."

Flushed with embarrassment, she ran after Jacqui and David.

"Listen, Mum's just reminded me. I left the oven on. The meat'll be horribly overdone, but the starter and desserts will be OK," she stammered, biting her bottom lip nervously.

Jacqui shook her head and laughed.

"It'll be *underdone*, Emma. I turned the oven off. I thought it would be safer."

"What will we do, then?" Emma didn't know whether to be delighted or dismayed.

They gazed at each other indecisively.

"If I could make a practical suggestion," David interrupted. "Why don't we all go out for a meal somewhere? I mean, it's a shame about the meal, but I'm sure Emma won't feel like rescuing it now."

"It's very kind of you." Emma was dubious. "But I feel I've let you both down so . . ."

They didn't seem to be getting anywhere. Celia, who had caught up with them in the middle of this discussion, stood and chuckled as they tried to reach an agreement.

"We could stand here all weekend while you lot carry on!

"Why don't you all come back to my place? I made a great big pot of soup today, and I'm sure I can rustle up a main course — even if it's just egg and chips. We can be there in five minutes. What do you say?"

Emma looked at her dinner guests in all their finery. What an end to their evening!

"That's a lovely idea." Jacqui smiled. "I can think of nothing nicer. Come on, Mrs Nicholls — you can lead the way."

"Thanks, Mum. It's an ideal solution," Emma echoed.

They all trooped out to the car-park. Celia clambered into her ageing Mini, and it spluttered into life while the others walked across to David's car.

THEY soon reached Celia's cottage. Celia parked by the front door, and hurried back to David.

"Right, just pull in there, under the tree," she instructed him.

"Now, come on in, everyone. You'll have to excuse the mess, but at least the kitchen is nice and cosy. The soup is just ready to warm up."

Opening the heavy, oak, front door, Celia led the way into the kichen, shifting a somnolent cat from the nearest chair.

"Now, just dump your coats, and come and sit down."

"Thanks, Mum." Emma sighed. "I don't know about David and Jacqui, but I'm famished. I've just remembered I forgot to have lunch!"

David took off his jacket and rolled up his sleeves.

"Now, what can I do to help, Mrs Nicholls? You said something about doing chips . . . ?"

"I'll help, too," Jacqui offered. "Have you two potato peelers?"

Emma looked on, bemused, as the impromptu meal prepared itself before her very eyes. It was ironic, she mused, that she'd spent all that time cooking — and now they were about to eat a meal that took less than half an hour to get ready!

Jacqui and David didn't seem to see anything incongruous about the situation. In fact, they were soon laughing and joking with Celia as though they'd known her for years.

Celia brought out a bottle of cider, and opened it with a flourish.

"It just so happens," she declared, "that I bought this for tomorrow. But I think we could all use it now, don't you?"

The rest of the evening — what there was left of it — went with a swing. It was nearly midnight when David reluctantly stood up and stretched contentedly.

"Well, Celia — it's been a lovely evening. I haven't had egg and chips like that in years. But I think we ought to be on our way now."

He looked across at Emma, whose eyelids were drooping unashamedly.

"Would you like to come home with us? I don't like to think of you going back to an empty house . . . "

"Well, I — "

"Oh, you poor love," Celia interrupted. "Thanks for offering, David, but Emma can stay here with me. Look — she's half asleep already."

Emma looked up wearily.

"Thanks, Mum. I can barely stay awake. Thanks for the thought, David."

"Well, we'll leave you in Celia's capable hands, then." Jacqui smiled.

"We'll phone you tomorrow evening to see how Robert is. 'Bye, Celia — thanks for everything!"

Celia waved them off, then locked up for the night.

"Now then, Emma. I'll just put the kettle on for a hot water-bottle, then I'll make up the spare bed for you. Don't just sit there at the table — make yourself comfy in an easy chair. I won't be long."

She hesitated. There was the slightest mischievous twinkle in her eyes.

"Let's just leave the washing-up, shall we? There's nothing that can't wait until the morning."

Emma knew she was being teased, but couldn't bring herself to rise to the bait.

"You're spoiling me rotten, Mum." She sighed, as she settled herself into the deepest, most comfortable chair. "And I'm loving every minute of it."

It was true. Soothed by Celia's motherly concern, she felt more relaxed than she had all week. I must tell Robert that, she reflected lazily.

As Celia reached across to fill the kettle, a solitary spoon clattered down from the heap of dirty dishes into the sink. She looked over her shoulder at Emma.

For a moment there was silence, before both women burst into helpless peals of laughter.

So there was a mountain of washing-up? Who cared? After all, what was a bit of clutter between friends? □

The Journey Home

MY journey into the past began with a phone call from my niece, Sue, bubbling over with excitement.

"Jim's got it!" she exclaimed. "After all these years! Oh, he's over the moon, well, naturally we all are, of course . . ."

It was hard to interrupt the flow. Her husband's long-awaited promotion to manager was wonderful news. Jim Roberts had looked the part from the age of twenty, but the bank had chosen to wait until he had thinning hair and a thickening waistline.

"Which branch is it to be?" I inquired, and a girlish chuckle rippled down the line. She sounded more like her own teenage daughter, Mandy.

"You'll never guess, Auntie Nell! We're going over the border, to Yorkshire — your old hometown, no less. Jim's the new manager at Broadley."

She chattered on, full of plans for their forthcoming move to the woollen town where I was born.

"And you're coming for a wee holiday," she insisted. "Just as soon as we've a roof over our heads."

"It's a very long way, dear. I'm not much of a traveller these days."

"There's an excellent through train," she replied firmly, "and Jim will meet you with the car in Leeds."

So, some months later, I found myself speeding southwards on an express train, returning to Broadley after more years than I cared to count. I was eagerly looking forward to seeing Sue's family in their new home, but deep inside was a queer, panicky feeling, a bit like going to the dentist.

Had Broadley changed a lot? Would anyone still remember me?

by MARIAN FARQUHARSON

What had happened to the little girl next door, Chrissie Long, and my very first boyfriend, Jack Smith, with his rugged face and slow, steady smile? I'd had no news of them in all these years. It was so incredibly easy to lose touch.

I WAS glad to have a friendly travelling companion. The pretty young woman opposite was accompanied by a haughty-looking Persian cat in a wicker travelling cage, protesting shrilly at its captivity.

"I must apologise for my friend." She grinned ruefully. "At least you're spared the rest of my menagerie. Back home there are three goats, two dogs and a parrot who's a great talker. Unfortunately it knows a few rather colourful words!"

She was on her way to visit her sister who, luckily, adored cats. I was soon chattering away, rather like her parrot, recounting my life story. How easy it is to talk to strangers.

"I was only seventeen when we moved from Broadley," I told her, "and I've never been back till now. All the people I knew as bright young things will be rather long in the tooth, I'm afraid."

"I've always believed you're as old as you *feel*, so maybe you'll find they haven't changed much at all." She smiled.

If only she were right! But an awful lot of water had flowed under the bridge. I thought of little Chrissie who'd lived next door, in a neat, little terraced house identical to all the others clustered round Crabtree's textile mill.

Our street was a bit special, for there were pots of colourful geraniums in nearly every window. Chrissie's father grew them as a hobby, winning medals galore, and gave cuttings to all the neighbours.

She was the baby sister I'd always longed for and never had. Six years my junior, from the day of her birth I'd regarded her as "mine." My first piece of proper knitting was a matinée jacket for Chrissie, riddled with dropped stitches, and I was actually permitted to wheel her out in her pram, the envy of my friends. And, oh, the sadness when I learned she had something wrong with her legs and would never walk properly.

Chrissie grew into a lovely, cheerful little girl, a perfect poppet with blue eyes and a mass of golden curls. Most of my spare time was spent reading aloud her favourite fairy-tales or playing quiet games, much more to my liking than rough and tumbles with my lively brothers.

We talked endlessly of what we'd do when we grew up. We fancied a little shop . . . or perhaps a thatched cottage with a duckpond and a pet donkey and a sign which said "Teas."

"You'll always be my very best friend," said Chrissie.

"Always," I agreed solemnly. But now, a lifetime later, the plain truth was that I hadn't the least idea what had happened to her.

MY friend with the cat said goodbye at York, in a flurry of bags and baskets. A tall young man from farther down our carriage rushed eagerly to assist. They stood together on the platform, gaily chatting, and waved vigorously as the train glided out of the station. I felt a little sad to lose sight of them.

Perhaps they would strike up a lasting friendship, even a romance, for who knew where a chance encounter could lead? At a similar age I had tumbled down a flight of steps, right into the arms of the law!

The young constable who picked me up, bruised but with no bones broken, seemed more unnerved than I was. In the fullness of time PC Charlie MacPherson had become my very dear husband, often joking that I'd fallen at his feet on purpose! Sadly, Charlie died a couple of years ago after a short illness, but I have so many happy memories he never seems far away.

The family were waiting for me at Leeds. I hugged Mandy and Sue in turn, then Jim, who looked extremely formal in a dark, pin-striped suit.

"Is it all right to hug bank managers in public?" I teased.

"Only if you're an old and valued customer," he responded solemnly, but his eyes were twinkling.

"You're having my bedroom, Auntie Nell," Mandy informed me. "Hope you don't mind a few pop stars on the walls, but the spare room's still under construction!"

"We've been waiting weeks for the fitted wardrobe." Sue groaned.

A half-hour's drive brought us to the outskirts of Broadley, and a new housing estate.

"This was open country when I was a girl," I told them. "All fields and woods, a popular haunt for courting couples."

Vividly I recalled a long-ago summer's afternoon, and emotional goodbyes to Jack Smith behind an oak tree. Such an ache in my heart there was, for my family was moving to the North of Scotland, and who knew when we'd meet again? I was late home for supper and earned a real ticking off, besides getting mud on my best white sandals.

Jim and Sue's new home was a charming bungalow with just enough garden to keep a bank manager busy at weekends. Mandy's room was bright and cheerful, with a huge rainbow painted across one wall. She assured me she enjoyed camping out in the guest-room.

"Mum's an old fusspot sometimes," she confided, fussing with her chewed fringe in the mirror. "Wasn't she ever the least bit way out?"

"Well, there was a time she favoured hair so long it used to dip into her soup. I'm sure I've some old snapshots somewhere . . ."

There was a tap at the door.

"Am I disturbing anything?" inquired Sue. "From the sound of the giggling, you're having a great time up here."

She waved the evening paper at me.

"Here's a bit of news. Grandad worked all his life at Crabtree's, didn't he? The old mill is being demolished, to make way for the new shopping centre they're building. The big chimney is to come down this Sunday afternoon."

Crabtree's mill! I grew up in the shadow of its massive stone buildings and soaring chimney-stack, reputedly the tallest in the West Riding. My father was a loom tuner, highly skilled, and his father and uncles before him had all worked at Crabtree's. Jack Smith, my long-ago heart-throb, was an apprentice there . . .

I walked to the window. "Can we see the chimney from here?"

"Just out of sight, I'm afraid."

"We're going to watch them blow it up, I hope?" Mandy's eyes were shining like stars. "Won't it be great!"

I pretended to agree, but inwardly I felt choked. Why couldn't they leave things alone? A familiar landmark was going to disappear for ever.

SUNDAY was hot and sunny, but the day had begun badly. Sue had a migraine and only wanted to be left in peace. For two pins I'd have called off the outing, but Jim and Mandy were keen to go, so we set off to secure a good vantage point.

At first I thought Jim was hopelessly lost, for I couldn't recognise my old haunts. A new motorway scythed through the town, with acres of grass embankments.

The police had cordoned off all the roads leading to the mill. Jim parked on some waste ground and we set off on foot. I tried to get

HIDDEN VILLAGES OF SCOTLAND

KETTINS (near Coupar Angus)

IT'S not often you'll meet a church belfry face to face before you reach its front door, but that's the way of it at Kettins.

You get a glimpse of this village, half-hidden by woodland, from the Coupar Angus road to the south. It's only a mile away and well worth going the traditional mile to see, with cottages and gardens forming a ring around the kirk, a lychgate and village green, a lively little burn, bridges, and this extra bell-tower I mentioned.

It so happened that when this belfry was being replaced by a new one, it was decided to preserve the old one, as it was a valuable part of the church's history, which can be traced back to the 13th century. So there the old massive 16th century Dutch bell remains on the green sward, beautifully inscribed with the names of the bell-founder and donor, and ready to ring out again if necessary. But how a

Dutch kirk bell came to be installed in a Scottish village kirk remains its secret.

In its earliest form, the meaning of Kettins is given as "Kathenes, of that thanage." Probably the original Gaelic name meant "place belonging to soldiers," yet it was connected with St Mary's Abbey at Coupar.

Little remains of that great Abbey now, but Kettins Kirk is very much alive and well!

my bearings, but it all looked so different. Where was Stanley Street and my old home?

"They've demolished a lot of the old houses, Auntie Nell, for this grand new shopping complex. Where exactly did you used to live?"

"I haven't the faintest idea," I confessed. "It seems to have vanished from the face of the earth."

Scores of people were converging on the high ground above Crabtree's, seeking a grandstand view.

"What if the chimney falls the wrong way?" Mandy said ghoulishly.

We found ourselves a good spot against a wall, and I scoured the crowd for a familiar face from the past. But I was surrounded by strangers.

An Indian woman nearby was wearing a rose-pink sari, richly embroidered with gold thread, like a princess in one of the fairy tales Chrissie used to love.

Down in the mill yard there was heightened activity. Demolition men in bright yellow helmets were scurrying to and fro. The sun shone relentlessly in a cloudless blue sky, and the tall chimney shimmered in the heat haze. I remembered another golden afternoon . . .

There were huge crowds, too, on that far-off gala occasion, to mark the opening of new weaving sheds. The mill was festooned with bunting, and the town band occupied a rather makeshift platform, looking uncomfortably hot in their dark uniforms. Old Alderman Crabtree, puffed up like a turkey cock, was well embarked on a long and boring speech. His voice droned on and on.

"Why doesn't the silly old duffer fall through the platform?" Jack Smith hissed in my ear.

"Shush, Jack," I reproved, stifling a giggle.

Little Chrissie, dressed in her Sunday best, turned round in her wheelchair.

"What did he say?" she demanded.

"Tell you later, sweetheart," I promised, ruffling her fair curls. I experienced one of those rare moments of sheer happiness when I could have burst for joy.

I was just seventeen and "walking out" with Jack. In a year or two, and no hurry, Jack would doubtless "pop the question" and I'd be showing off a sparkly ring on my third finger. He was reckoned quite a catch and, more importantly, Mum and Dad liked him. Not exactly handsome, mind, with his rather craggy features, but when he smiled that slow, steady smile my knees turned to jelly.

My daydream went on and on, leading to a fairytale wedding with me in a bridal gown all sleek and shimmering, like that sateen in the dressmaker's window at a staggering three and eleven the yard! Chrissie would be our bridesmaid, of course, wheelchair and all. We'd trim it up really prettily with bows of fluttering ribbons. It would be her big day, too . . .

Back in the present, I felt suddenly chilled despite the sunshine. That gala day had been one of my last happy memories of Broadley. Dad had died suddenly and my mother took my young brothers and myself away to a new life with our grandparents in the Highlands.

At first I missed Broadley desperately, and especially Chrissie and Jack, and I wrote long, newsy letters to them both. Neither were great letterwriters, though that's no excuse for me. Gradually the correspondence dwindled, became an exchange of Christmas greetings. Inevitably, the gap became too wide to bridge.

Three o'clock chimed from the clock tower, and there was a sudden unearthly hush.

"Put your fingers in your ears," hissed Mandy.

I held my breath. The muffled roar of an explosion rent the air and, for a nerve-tingling moment, the old chimney stood firm. Then, almost in slow motion, it seemed to sway and crumble, collapsing like a house of cards in a swirling cloud of dust.

A great cheer rang out, echoing round the valley. Everyone shouted and clapped. Mandy gave me a great bear hug.

"Wasn't that just great!" She sighed.

I found myself fighting back tears, overcome with emotion. This was the end of an era, the last page turned in the book. The skyline was strangely empty. It was as if the chimney and all my youthful memories had never been there at all.

The crowds began to disperse.

"I'm going to fetch the car nearer, save your legs a bit," announced Jim, ever the practical one. Away he went, leaving Mandy and me perched on a convenient low wall to wait. It was freezing cold.

"Let's have some hot coffee," Mandy suggested. "I saw a van selling refreshments earlier. I'll run along and get them."

THE next bit is rather hazy. I sat on my own for what seemed ages, wishing Jim or Mandy would return. Perhaps I should try to find them. I set off in the direction Mandy had taken, making slow progress across the rough ground. I was feeling very shaky. All at once I stumbled and fell, and my bulky handbag flew from my grasp.

"Hey, are you all right?" A young lad of eleven or so, with a mop of luxuriant fair curls, hovered anxiously, and helped me to my feet.

"Just a bit shaken, that's all," I said. "Luckily the ground's fairly soft."

He swiftly retrieved the contents of my bag, which had spilled open in the fall.

"My gran's bag is just like yours, bursting with things," he remarked cheerily. "I often carry it for her and it weighs a ton!"

"I'm sure she finds you a great help." I smiled.

He took my arm with an old-fashioned courtesy.

"She calls me her extra legs . . . Doesn't it look funny now the chimney's gone?"

"It does rather," I agreed.

"Gran refused to come and watch. She likes things to stay the way they are." He regarded me curiously. "D'you live round here?"

"I used to, when I was a girl," I told him, "but my home's in Scotland, up in the North. I'm spending a wee holiday with my niece."

He grinned and something tugged fleetingly at my memory.

"Broadley's a funny place for a holiday. We're going to the seaside. I get a bit tired of building sandcastles with my little sister, but Dad says he might take me water-skiing this year . . ."

Suddenly I spotted Mandy heading towards us, bearing three cups of coffee.

"Sorry I've been such an age," she apologised. "The queue stretched for miles!"

"This is my great-niece," I told my young friend, "and she's brought you a little reward for your kindness. Do you like coffee?"

He nodded eagerly. I felt sure Jim wouldn't mind forgoing his!

THE rest of my holiday flew by. We had a lovely day exploring the beautiful Dales, with a meal at a five-hundred-year-old farm-house with beehives in the garden. Then there was an evening barge cruise, wining and dining on the Leeds/Liverpool Canal.

"Better than Venice!" Mandy declared.

Jim did his best to trace Chrissie and Jack, following various leads which all petered out. I was very disappointed, but tried to shrug it off. The grand reunion had been too much to hope for.

All too soon I was boarding the train for the homeward journey, leaving Broadley and my dear ones behind.

It seemed a long, tedious journey, but at last I was home. It was only a short taxi ride from the station, and the driver kindly carried my case up the path.

"Shall I wait while you unlock the door?" he suggested thoughtfully.

"No thank you, I can manage fine," I assured him, secretly dreading that chill emptiness of a house unoccupied for a couple of weeks, and facing afresh, as I always did, the fact that Charlie wasn't there to welcome me home.

The accumulated post lying on the doormat was soon dealt with. I left one crisp, white envelope till last, intrigued by the unfamiliar handwriting and the fact that my address was incomplete. There was just my name and postcode.

D*EAR Nell,* the long letter began, Please forgive me if I'm writing to the wrong person, only I'm certain it was you who met my grandson, Danny, the day Crabtree's chimney was blown up.

Enclosed is your bus pass, which he says you must have dropped when you fell on the waste ground. (Hope the address finds you.) Danny told us he met a nice lady and helped pick up her things, then later he found the pass lying in some grass. I'm sure it's you from the photo.

Do you remember me living next door to you when I was a youngster? I was so sad when you moved away. I know we wrote a few times, but somehow I managed to lose your address.

Maybe you'll be wondering what happened to me when I grew up. You couldn't guess in a hundred years, so I'll tell you. I married your old flame, Jack Smith. Doesn't life work out in funny ways?

After you moved away, Jack didn't seem to bother much with girls, and all the time I had this secret crush on him. Well, the years went by and I grew up, and Jack still kept calling at our house. Dad used to think it was his precious geraniums he was coming to see!

Then one day he asked if I'd fancy marrying him, and I thought it was some awful kind of joke, with me never being able to walk more than a few steps. But he actually meant it, and at last he persuaded me it was me he wanted to marry, not a pair of legs!

So that was that, and we had a wonderful wedding. My dress was white brocade and I wore an antique lace veil that Jack's mother had worn at her wedding, and I upset Dad something awful by refusing to carry a bouquet of geraniums!

So there we are, Nell dear, and I must stop rambling on, except to tell you that Jack and I have a son, Ronald, who runs a small garage.

Ron took his time about settling down and they have two youngsters, Danny and little Sheila. You've met Danny, of course. He's the image of his granddad but he's got my curls. Wasted on a lad, don't you think?

Jack joins me in sending love and all good wishes to you. He says he's never forgotten you, but has had to put up with me instead! We moved to our "country place" when Jack retired. D'you remember how we used to dream about a cottage with a duckpond and a pet donkey and a sign that said "Teas?" Well, at last I've got the cottage, and Jack says I should put the "Teas" sign up, for folk are always calling by for a cuppa!

Do please drop a line and give us all your news.

Love from Chrissie.

My eyes were moist as I re-read the letter for the third time. I've always had a good cry at weddings, and though Chrissie's was so long ago, surely it wasn't too late to enjoy a little weep? Chrissie and Jack, just imagine! I was so tremendously happy for them both.

I was humming "The Wedding March" as I put the kettle on for a welcome cup of tea. And to think I might never have seen them again, if I hadn't had that silly fall. I smiled to myself, knowing what Charlie would have said.

"Ay, you make quite a habit of it, lass! Some things *never* change." □

Noises In The Night

IF I were a dog I'd fiercely bark,
At menacing noises in the dark.

If I were a cat I'd yowl and screech,
At the moon beyond my reach.

If I were an owl, while in pursuit
Of prey to eat, I'd loudly hoot.

Were I a hedgehog, my nightly trail,
Would find me snuffling worm and snail.

If I were a small and hungry mouse,
I'd squeak and scuttle about the house.

But at night I just lie snoring,
Not allowed to go exploring!

— Christine Peters.

by
ELSPETH
MANLEY

The Perfect Compromise

AS I walked back from the letterbox, I smiled inwardly.

Things could have been so different — but I don't regret the way they've turned out.

I can remember the argument as though it were yesterday.

"Why must you be so cautious, Debbie?" Pete had stormed.

"Not cautious — just using my commonsense. What's the point in starting out with a massive mortgage hanging over us?"

"I just want the best we can afford. Wouldn't you prefer a house to a flat?"

He was furious with me, but I couldn't help the way I felt.

My mother had always struggled to make ends meet. If I had one ambition in life, it was to avoid that kind of struggle. I didn't want to have to watch every penny just to live in a bigger house.

I hated the way our relationship had become so strained. Was it all going to go sour, just a few months before the wedding?

I'd promised to visit Great-Aunt Lily that weekend. It was her eightieth birthday, and I'd already baked her a special cake.

Pete had agreed to drive me over to Brixmouth, but I changed my mind and decided to go alone. It would give us both some breathing space.

I got an early train and settled down to read a magazine on the journey.

It didn't take me long to get engrossed in a story. I hardly noticed the movements around me, as passengers got on at the next station.

I CAME back to reality as someone tapped my shoulder.

"It *is* Debbie Mortimer, isn't it?"

I stared at him. The tall, bearded man was waiting for me to recognise him. Although he looked familiar, I couldn't place him . . .

"I'm sorry. You'll have to help me . . ." I apologised.

"I'm Terry Noble. The beard's a good disguise, isn't it?"

"Terry! Of course! What must you think of me? What are you doing with yourself these days?"

I was struggling to hide my embarrassment. Terry had been my first proper boyfriend when we were both awkward, shy teenagers.

"I finished university a couple of years ago. Now I'm an accountant. I've been up in London, but I came back to Plymbury earlier this year. What about you?"

"Still in the bank. But I'm not a cashier any more — I got promoted."

"That's great! Are you still living at home?"

I hesitated. I'd have to tell him about Pete, but I wasn't in the mood for being congratulated — not with the dreadful atmosphere between Pete and me at the moment.

"Yes, I'm still living with Mum. But not for much longer. Do you remember Pete Sinclair? He was in the year above us at school."

"Oh, yes. We were in the same rugby team." He smiled, remembering.

"That's him. Well, we're engaged to be married."

"Congratulations! When's the wedding?" His voice was friendly and I found myself relaxing.

"March. The only problem is, we haven't got anywhere to live yet," I admitted.

"So you'll have been house-hunting, then?"

I smiled ruefully.

"Well — no. We're still trying to decide what we're looking for. Anyway, enough about me. How about you?"

He grinned.

"Still footloose and fancy-free. I've got a nice little flat on the edge of town. I'm getting on fine. You wouldn't believe it, but I'm quite a good cook now!"

Remembering his early attempts at Spanish omelettes at school, I first couldn't help laughing.

"You amaze me! You must have put in a lot of practice. I prefer baking, myself." I nodded towards the carrier bag beside me.

"I'm taking a birthday cake to my aunt today. I would show you, but it's all wrapped up."

Terry stood up.

"Talking of food, I need a coffee. Can I get you anything from the buffet?"

"I've got plenty of coffee in my flask. You're welcome to have some. I wouldn't mind a sandwich, though, if you're offering to get something."

He nodded.

"Sounds a fair exchange. See you in a minute."

He smiled as he returned to his seat a while later.

"It's really good seeing you again, Debbie. I've lost touch with most of the old crowd from school. Do you still see any of them?"

"Oh, from time to time. Pete plays rugby with several of them. You should go along some time. They're always crying out for good players."

He looked interested.

"I might just do that. Where do they meet?"

By the time I'd explained about the club, and where they'd been playing, the train wasn't far from my destination.

"Mine's the next stop, Terry. Look, I'll give you Pete's number — give him a ring. I'm sure you'll get something sorted out. Perhaps we'll meet again."

He reached across and patted my arm as I stood up to leave.

"Take care, Debbie. I hope your aunt enjoys her cake! See you!"

I WAS still thinking about him as I walked the short distance from the station to Aunt Lily's.

He was charming and good looking, with his thick, dark hair and that well-groomed beard. I couldn't imagine that he'd be short of girlfriends.

Aunt Lily looked frail, but her welcome was as warm as ever.

"Come on in, love. The kettle's not long off the boil. But where's Pete? Not ill, I hope?"

"We had a bit of a disagreement yesterday," I admitted. "Nothing major — but this business of finding somewhere to live is really getting to us. I thought we could do with a weekend to cool down."

She was sympathetic.

"Quite right, dear. Well, never mind — maybe *I* can cheer you up while you're here. I'm sure it'll all work out in the end."

When I left to go home that evening, I felt considerably calmer. And, just as important, we'd celebrated Aunt Lily's birthday in grand style. The cake went down a treat, and Lily herself had done some baking, too.

As I left, she kissed me warmly.

"Let me know how you and Pete get on. You know I'm always at the end of a phone if you need someone to talk to."

By the time I saw Pete again, the storm had blown over — on the surface, at least. But it was more of a truce than a lasting settlement.

If I had done one thing right, though, it was giving his phone number to Terry. Pete was delighted to hear he was back in town, and reminded me that he would be an asset to any team.

We saw quite a lot of Terry that winter. He didn't just join the club for the rugby, either. The social events were soon as much a part of his calendar as they were of ours.

Mind you, if I'd thought I'd be spending cosy evenings at the club, discussing times gone by with Terry, I was totally mistaken. Every time he came to the club, he appeared with a different girl, each one more glamorous than the last.

"That man's going places," Pete observed. "And he's not in any hurry to settle down, is he?"

I smiled across at him.

Pete's comment was entirely without rancour, and I admired him for that. Like me, he had a good, steady job. We'd never have the lifestyle that Terry was aiming for.

We still hadn't solved the problem of somewhere to live, though. With only three months until the wedding, it was something that had to be sorted out sooner or later.

But Christmas was fast approaching. We agreed to let the matter drop until the New Year. There was too much to do before that.

THE rugby club party was, by tradition, the highlight of the year. It was an old-established custom that girlfriends and wives did the catering and got the hall decorated beforehand.

We were all surprised when Terry turned up halfway through the morning. He was on his own, too, for once.

"Hello, ladies. Do you need a hand with anything?" he volunteered, smiling.

"We certainly do!" One of the girls sighed. "There's a whole mountain of paper chains to put up, for a start. And then there's the mistletoe . . ."

"Leave it to me." He grinned. "Now, where's the ladder?"

We left him to it. There was still plenty to do in the kitchen.

It must have been half an hour later when I went back through into the hall with the tablecloths and napkins. Terry was just climbing down from pinning the last decoration to the rafters.

"Hey, that's fantastic, Terry!" I wasn't just flattering him, either.

He stood back to survey the effect.

"Mmm, not bad, though I say it myself. Just one thing, though. Can you come over here a minute?"

Mystified, I went across to where he was standing.

"What's up?"

"Nothing. I just want to see if this works."

"If *what* works?"

He looked at me quizzically, then took me into his arms and kissed me.

Taken by surprise, I was almost frozen for a moment. Then I pushed him away, gently but firmly.

"What's the matter, Debbie? Relax — it's Christmas. See — I've put the mistletoe up!"

Sure enough, there it was — a whole bundle of the stuff. How could I have missed it?

"It might be Christmas, but that doesn't give you the right to take advantage of me!" I spluttered. "Besides, what would Pete say?"

"Pete doesn't have to know. Anyway, I thought you and Pete weren't getting on well. People are saying . . ."

"I don't care what they're saying." My voice was rising.

"Come on, Debbie! I thought you still had a soft spot for me. Look — come for a drink with me some evening. Just for old times' sake. You were friendly enough when I bumped into you on the train."

I felt my cheeks burning.

"I don't think that would be a good idea. Thanks for your help this morning, Terry, but I think we'll be able to manage the rest of the preparations now," I told him coldly.

He turned to go, then looked back at me.

"I'll be at the Black Bull next Tuesday night. Please come."

"I don't think so." I shook my head. "'Bye, Terry."

I went back to join the girls in the kitchen. My emotions were in turmoil, but I didn't want to talk about what had just happened.

I managed to get through the rest of the morning, joining in the usual banter and general chit-chat.

Then I fled home, hoping I'd get an hour to myself that afternoon. There was a letter I'd have to write, and the sooner the better.

It was the most difficult one I've ever written. It's two years now since I wrote it, and a lot of water has passed under the bridge — but I could still tell you, word for word, what went into it.

But it doesn't upset me any more. And, you know, I think I deserve full marks for diplomacy.

Not only did Terry apologise for making a pass at me that day, but he was big enough not to let it spoil his friendship with Pete and me.

That explains why I was smiling as I came away from the letterbox just now. I'd just posted our acceptance to attend Terry's wedding — he did settle down eventually — but that wasn't the only thing making me smile.

I was just reflecting that everything had turned out right for Pete and me in the end, too.

We'd reached the perfect compromise when we found our first home. The modest terraced house was not too expensive, but big enough for our latest acquisition.

I looked down and adjusted the lacy parasol. From under it, a cheeky little face gurgled up at me contentedly. Baby Lily was the perfect seal on a very happy marriage. □

The Farmer And His Wife

by John Taylor

IT was a Sunday evening, not late, but Anne had closed the curtains. She says it's more homely that way.

We had been watching "Songs of Praise," and enjoyed joining in some of the hymns we knew.

We switched off the TV set after that.

Anne looked across at me and asked, "What's amusing you, John?"

I didn't realise I had a smile on my face.

We had had, for a change, a beautiful high tea, as lunch had been light.

Yet it was often the done thing when we were young. It was one of the items served in that high tea that aroused memories which brought a smile to my face.

I'll tell you about the tea first.

Anne found herself with the remains of a pressed tongue. She cut it into small pieces, made a white sauce and added some parsley. With creamed potatoes and buttered carrots, it was really delicious.

It was that beautiful meal Anne had served up on that cold Sunday night which made me smile — the tongue part, to be exact.

WE hadn't long been married when I learned a lesson from Anne, one that has stayed with me for ever.

"When you're in the butcher's, John, ask for an ox tongue out of brine," she told me.

I did as requested.

"Sorry, John, I haven't any in brine, but I'm sure Anne will find this fresh tongue to her liking," he said.

I should have thanked him and said no, but at that time I didn't know the difference between a tongue out of brine and a fresh tongue. To hear Anne lecture me that evening, there's as much difference as between chalk and cheese.

One out of brine — your butcher may say, if he's posh — is a pickled tongue which has been soaked in brine. Anne maintains it has a better flavour and colour than a fresh one.

Anne presses her ox tongue. It's a fiddling business but well worthwhile if you price a few slices of tongue in a shop.

I was going into Kingsbarns one day when Anne said, "Oh John, drop this into Mrs — " — an old soul who had only her pension.

"This" was a plate with three large pieces of tongue wrapped in a polythene bag.

"Thank Anne, John," the old body asked me. "It looks beautiful, and must have cost a fortune."

When I told her Anne pressed it herself, she was amazed.

"NO, I won't go to any trouble, just a sandwich."

That was the end of a long conversation on the phone by Anne.

"I've asked Clare and Ian to come for a snack tonight," she told me.

I always thought a sandwich was something between two pieces of bread — but you live and learn with Anne.

She made what she called an open sandwich.

The base was a piece of brown bread, then there was another piece cut across into four triangles. Put these at the side of the other piece. Oh, I forgot, spread butter on them.

Add slices of tongue, then put sliced tomatoes, boiled eggs and lettuce plus anything else you want.

Anne really did make it look appetising.

I was proud of her.

"Anne, you said just a sandwich," Clare reminded her.

How we laughed that Sunday evening about tongues out of brine.

Memories are marvellous. Anne and I have many which we enjoy sharing with you.

IN THE KITCHEN with ANNE AND JOHN TAYLOR

TURKEY AND BROCCOLI FLAN

4 oz. (100 g) wholemeal pastry

4 oz. (100 g) cooked turkey, diced

2 oz. (50 g) broccoli spears

4 oz. (100 g) cream cheese

3 tablespoonfuls (45 ml) mayonnaise

2 oz. (50 g) Cheddar cheese, grated

5 tablespoonfuls (75 ml) milk

Salt and pepper, to taste

Pre-heat oven to 350 deg. F., 180 deg. C., Gas Mark 4. Line a 6 in. (15 cm) flan case with pastry and bake blind, in the centre of the oven, for 15 minutes.

Place turkey and broccoli in base of flan.

Beat together cream cheese and mayonnaise. Add Cheddar cheese and continue to beat well. Gradually add milk then season.

Spoon on top of turkey and broccoli. Bake in the centre of the oven, at the same temperature, until golden brown.

Serves 4.

CAULIFLOWER AND TURMERIC SOUP

1 oz. (25 g) butter

1 onion, chopped

2 carrots, grated

8 oz. (225 g) cauliflower, broken into florets

2 tomatoes, chopped

A small piece of turnip, diced

4 oz. (100 g) red lentils, washed and soaked

½ teaspoonful turmeric

2 tablespoonfuls oatmeal

½ teaspoonful mixed herbs

1 pint (568 ml) vegetable stock

1½ pints (900 ml) milk

Salt and pepper, to taste

To Garnish. —
Fresh parsley, chopped

Melt butter in a large saucepan. Add vegetables, tomatoes and lentils. Cook for 5 minutes, stirring occasionally.

Add turmeric, oatmeal and herbs. Cook for a further 2 minutes.

Pour in stock and milk. Season. Bring to the boil and simmer for 35 minutes.

Liquidise, if liked, and serve garnished with parsley.

Serves 4.

"WHAT'S all this . . . ?" Peter Burns demanded shortly, surveying the chaos in the kitchen and hall of his normally immaculate home.

Mary Burns winced. This was just what she had been dreading. Her husband, retired now from his life-long job in the local mill, had always been a stickler for having "everything in its place . . ."

He seemed to have become even more rigid in his outlook over the last few months, almost to the extent of expecting her household routine to run like clockwork.

She'd never expected his retirement to be an easy change for either of them. They had shared what she thought of now as an old-fashioned sort of marriage. He had been very much head of the family, and the breadwinner — and she had stayed at home, caring for and bringing up their four sons.

She had made it her business to see that their home was kept the way she knew Peter liked to see it — shining and tidy.

Naturally, if there was a big family decision to be made, like their eldest son, Alistair's move to England, it was her husband who took the initiative. But the small things — bumped knees and simple day-to-day caring — had been Mary's job.

And now Alistair was back, complete with wife and baby. He'd arrived nearly two hours later than Mary had expected. Mary had shooed her husband off to his bowling club a few hours ago, hoping Alistair and his family would be unpacked before Peter arrived back.

It was heaven to have Peter out from under her feet every now and again.

And if she did feel slightly guilty at such a thought, at least it meant that he was spared the sort of domestic bustle and stir which was most guaranteed to irritate him. More and more recently, she'd been dismayed to find that his temper was inclined to be short, especially when things weren't going as smoothly as he thought they should be.

"Method!" he'd exclaimed recently, when he found Mary in the middle of pulling out the

:ontents of the glory-hole :upboard under the stairs.

He had shaken his head at ıer, while making for the back loor and the pristine order of ıis potting-shed.

"A proper method for tackling ıny job is what you need. You nake work for yourself the way 'ou do things!"

Mary had always been very :alm and easy in her emperament but, on that ›ccasion, she had been startled o find herself biting her ongue, to prevent the tart reply vhich had risen instantly to her ips.

As the back door banged behind him, she took a deep breath. There was no point in reminding him that if Alistair and his wife and little daughter were to stay with them for the month it was going to take to get their new house ready, then that meant a giant clear-out of all the cupboards.

After all, it had been Peter's idea to invite them, when they'd learned their house wouldn't be ready on time.

ɔy
JENNIFER FRANCES

NEVER TOO OLD TO LEARN

ALISTAIR'S move back to Scotland meant promotion for him, and more money.

"He's done well for himself," Peter had said. "And we have the room, with all of them gone, working away. It'll give us a chance to get to know our English daughter-in-law, since we've hardly met her, except at the wedding."

He'd shot a teasing glance at Mary.

"You won't mind getting your only grandchild under your wing for a while, will you, love?"

"I'd jump at the chance." She'd smiled. She'd love the opportunity to welcome Carrie and little Morag to the village, but worried they would upset Peter's routines.

"Well, will I write and ask them to come?" he'd demanded. "Are they welcome?"

"Indeed they are!" she'd exclaimed. "More than welcome . . ."

And I, she had added to herself, will do everything to make sure they stay that way. This house will be organised within an inch of its life, before they ever get here!

So, she had set to with a will, and on the day they were to arrive, the largest spare room was bright and waiting, the airing cupboard had been re-organised, so that there was room for piles of nappies, and new curtains hung crisply at the window of what would become the little girl's nursery.

Mary had been prepared for everything — except a hold-up on the motorway which meant that her guests had arrived a bare thirty minutes ago, tired, hungry, and inclined to be cross.

Alistair was busy hauling in what seemed to be an incredible amount of brightly-coloured bits of what had to be baby things.

Mary looked around at the steadily-growing heaps of bags and cases, and shuddered as her husband tramped heavily into the middle of the mess. Of course, it wasn't his fault. He was, as always, dead on time, ready for his lunch.

By now, she'd planned that everything should be cleared away, the baby's cot put together upstairs — perhaps even with the baby in it, sleeping sweetly! — order restored, and the smell of a special lunch filling the house.

GOOD heavens, lass!" Peter barked. "What's all this? It's like a circus in here . . ." He broke off as a child's wail came from the direction of the sitting-room where the pram had been placed.

"Where's Carrie?" he demanded, looking round for his daughter-in-law. "That child is tired out by the sound of it. And where's Alistair? Why isn't he doing something about all this?"

At that moment, Mary felt like nothing more than howling and turned on her husband.

"He is doing something!" she snapped. "He's busy adding to the chaos, every time he comes back from the car!"

With that, the door opened with a bump, as Alistair pushed it from the other side with the edge of the case in his hand.

"Mind the paintwork, son!" Peter told him. "Here, let me take that. I knew I should have stayed at home this morning, but the General here had all her plans laid, and wouldn't be interfered with."

To Mary's indignation, he nodded in her direction, before greeting his son properly.

"The General!" she repeated. "I like that. At least this was all organised properly . . . with method," she finished bitterly, "even if the roadworks messed everything up."

Her husband shot her a look.

"Oh, I asked for that one. I've been waiting to get it flung back at me."

He turned to his son and, to Mary's growing fury, had the gall to chuckle.

"I was foolish enough to accuse your mum of doing a household job with no proper method to it. I didn't mean anything by it, but I knew I hadn't heard the end of it."

Alistair, rummaging through the opened suitcase on the floor, glanced up at his parents.

"You two been rubbing each other up the wrong way? Been spending all your time together in the house, have you?" he asked shrewdly.

His gaze took in his mother's flushed cheeks, and his father's rueful expression.

"Yes. I thought so. You're both strong characters, in your own different ways. It takes a lot of caring to make the sort of adjustments that are needed for a happy retirement . . ."

His hand closed in triumph on a scrap of faded cot-blanket.

"Ah!" He waved it like a banner, as the determined wail gathered to an ear-splitting howl next door. "This is what is causing all the fuss. Morag's precious comfort blanket — it must have got pushed in here, at the bottom, out of sight. She won't settle without it, as you can hear!"

"Leave that, son, we'll get it all upstairs later." Peter gestured at the contents of the case spilling out across the hall.

Alistair raised his brows at his father.

"If you're sure . . . ?"

To Mary's amazement, his father grinned at him.

"Away with you! What does a bit of muddle matter, when you've just come home? Let's go in and help Carrie, before the poor lass is deafened by wee Morag." He led the way to the sitting-room.

"Come on then, where's the wee girl with the best lungs in Scotland?"

Carrie, struggling to calm a sturdy, fifteen-month-old toddler, was glad to hand the child into her father-in-law's open arms.

"Whew . . ." She took a deep breath in relief. "She gets heavier every day.

"Hello, Dad." She smiled.

CRATHES CASTLE and GARDENS, GRAMPIAN : J CAMPBELL KERR

Peter settled the baby in the crook of his arm with an assured hand.

"There," he said, giving her the well-worn piece of cloth, "that's what you wanted, isn't it? My, I can see you're a determined wee thing, as well as a bonnie one.

"Well," he murmured, the howls instantly banished as Morag cuddled her comfort blanket, "the bonnie bit you get from your granny, as well as your mum. But the determined bit — mabye I'm a little to blame for that!"

Mary could only look on in amazement. Peter had been a loving father — no-one could have cared more about his boys, but nursing fretful babies had never been his style.

PETER continued jiggling Morag.

"Now, young lady," he told the child solemnly, "I'm your grandpa. And you and I are going to get along just fine, when we've got to know each other a bit better.

"We'll both have to learn to not be so set on having our own way! Sometimes, you know, you have to care enough to learn to be a bit less demanding — a bit more flexible . . ."

His words were murmured to the child, but the look he shot over the head now nuzzling into his pullover was directed at his wife.

"And let me tell you something — some of us take a lot of teaching, when we've got so set in our ways! Well, you're going to learn from me, wee lass, because that's what grandpas are for."

Mary felt her eyes fill. She knew he was offering an apology to her — for all the niggling little moments, since he'd retired, when they had both been less patient, less caring, than they should have been.

"And grannies," she managed to get out. "Grannies teach caring, and learn from it too, I hope."

The look that passed between them, over the head of the contented, now sleepily murmuring child, said everything.

Mary realised she'd been too ready to look for faults — she'd felt crowded, almost threatened by having Peter at home all day.

She was too used to having her own way at home — hadn't she been just as inflexible as Peter?

◄ p103.

CRATHES CASTLE AND GARDENS

ONE of the most visited properties of the National Trust for Scotland in the north-east of Scotland, this is the ancestral home of the Burnetts of Leys. One of its great treasures is the Horn of Leys, a horn of fluted ivory with four bands of gilt and three crystals. It is believed to be the original horn which symbolised Robert the Bruce's granting of the land of Leys in the ancient royal forest of Drum to Alexander Burnard in 1323. The gardens consist of a series of small, interlinked gardens, and are worth seeing at any time of the year. They are surrounded by a magnificent yew hedge which was planted in 1702.

She leaned over Morag and kissed Peter gently on the cheek.

"We both care enough to try again, from the beginning," she vowed.

"Aye, love." He smiled, looking round — at little Morag, Carrie, Alistair and Mary.

"We're a family, with an awful lot to give each other. I promise I'll try to be the best grandfather possible!

"I know times have changed, and it'll be hard for me to change with them. But I know nowadays dads do a lot more for their children than I did. Well, Alistair, if you're willing to teach me, I'm willing to learn . . ."

Carrie smiled at him.

"I think that's wonderful!" she exclaimed. "I'm sure you're going to be so good for Morag. She's going to be a very lucky little girl!"

Mary felt proud enough to burst. She thought she knew everything there was to know about Peter — yet now . . .

"I think it's just wonderful, too," she assured him, and they all looked towards Alistair, who seemed to be hesitating.

He stood up, rubbing his hand over his hair in the gesture so familiar from his childhood, whenever he was in doubt about anything.

"It's great, Dad," he said seriously. "Really great. Honestly. It's just . . ."

His father looked him straight in the eye.

"Just what, son?" he asked.

"Well, just . . . if you really mean it, then I think I ought to start by teaching you what I would do for Morag, right this minute." And his grin hovered at the corner of his mouth, as his father nodded vigorously.

"Of course I mean it. Why wouldn't I? Mary, do you know what he's talking about?"

Mary's bewilderment dissolved finally, in a chuckle, as she saw Carrie rummage in a neat hold-all beside her.

"He means, Grandpa, that your granddaughter needs her nappy changing!"

The stricken look of panic on Peter's face was priceless. Mary laughed until tears came to her eyes.

"Oh, how I wish I had a camera," she finally spluttered. "What a way to have to start. Or are you backing out now, love?"

"No-one would blame you," Carrie assured him between giggles, and Alistair waited, grinning, for his judgment.

"Oh no," the proud grandpa said. "I've got my dander up now. I'm not backing out. Come on, Alistair, you'd better instruct me on this one!"

And off he went, to change a nappy for the first time in his life.

Carrie crossed to her mother-in-law, to envelop her in a warm hug.

"That's quite a husband you have there," she said softly.

Mary nodded, smiling.

"Yes," she answered. "Yes, he is." □

Growing Up Is

by
ROXY
MEALING

Hard To Do

LIZZIE BROWN sat cross-legged on the bed, listening to the church bells. A breeze ruffled the branches of the oak tree outside her window, casting bright dancing sunshine across the room.

Lizzie loved it. She loved this time of year when the breeze carried a hint of warmth and promised summer.

"Are you up yet, Lizzie?"

"Yes, Mum!" She jumped off the bed.

And there, hanging on the outside of the wardrobe so it didn't get crushed or creased, was her dress.

In the room next door, she could hear her sister singing.

Rosie was in love, about to get married, and always singing.

Lizzie leaned on the window-sill and breathed in the fresh country air. She wasn't so much losing a sister, as gaining a bedroom!

Once Rosie was off and away, she'd be free of this tiny room. She'd have room to expand and breathe . . .

When her friends came round, they wouldn't all have to squash together on the bed, getting in each other's way, digging with elbows and knees.

"Haven't you had your shower yet, Lizzie?" her mother said, poking her head round the door.

"Come on. I know you're not exactly keen to be a bridesmaid, but this is Rosie's big day and . . ."

"I'm on my way." Lizzie grinned.

"And don't forget to use soap!"

Lizzie stood under the warm jets of water and smothered herself in Rosie's shower gel. She had two older sisters, Rosie and Jessica. Jessica had married last year and now it was Rosie's turn; she was marrying Matt.

She had managed to get out of being a bridesmaid for Jessica by breaking her leg. Well, she hadn't broken it on purpose, it was one of the more pleasant side-effects of a rather horrible accident.

She'd fallen out of a tree. Her parents said she should have been a boy. Lizzie thought so, too. It was no fun being a girl.

"COME on, Lizzie, hurry yourself." Her mother chivvied her over breakfast. "I'll give you a hand to get into your dress when you're ready."

Lizzie pulled a face. She couldn't help it.

"Come on now! You'll look lovely."

The only time Lizzie ever wore a skirt was to school. The minute she was home, the skirt was tossed aside and her jeans rescued from the pile of clothes she stored on the floor.

Upstairs, she stood in front of the dress. It was pink trimmed with white. Everyone said how pretty it was.

"I'll look like an Austrian blind," she grumbled to herself. "I don't know why Rosie couldn't elope and have done with it. Or get married in the West Indies like her friend Fiona."

"I'll do your hair!" Her mother breezed in and pushed Lizzie down at the dressing-table.

"Ow, ouch, awww," she protested as the tangles were teased out.

"You want to look beautiful, don't you?"

"No."

Lizzie hadn't seen herself wearing the dress. She'd tried it on, standing on a chair, when Mrs Bellingham had come to do the fitting. But she'd refused even to glance at her reflection.

She knew how she'd look. Like Lizzie Brown in a silly dress. No — not me. The dress would look all right. . . but her head at the top would look all wrong!

The rest of the morning saw the house in a state of organised uproar. Her mother dashed from one bedroom to another, getting the bridesmaids ready, helping Rosie into her dress, making sure the flowers had been delivered.

Her father stayed downstairs, keeping well out of the way. He'd been practising for weeks now. He didn't want to make the same mistake he'd made at Jessica's wedding.

"Who gives this woman?" the vicar had asked.

"Me!" Lizzie's dad had bellowed.

"I do," he said now, calmly and certainly. "I do. I do."

Once they were all ready, they assembled in her mother's bedroom. The other bridesmaids — two cousins of the groom — looked chocolate-box pretty and Rosie looked simply beautiful, glowing and radiant.

Lizzie swallowed the lump in her throat. Next to them, she must look awkward and clumsy and distinctly unfeminine.

She avoided looking in the mirror.

Her father passed the bedroom door on his way to the bathroom.

"I do," he said as he went by. "I do, I do."

The dress felt cool and soft against her skin.

"Cheer up, Lizzie," her mother said, handing her her posy of orange blossom. "It'll be over before you know it."

Lizzie gripped the flowers. Her hands felt hot and sweaty. She wished with all her heart that Rosie hadn't insisted on her being a bridesmaid.

She wished she'd stopped biting her nails, so they looked as smooth and pretty as Rosie's . . . She wished . . . she wished she was pretty, too.

THE cars arrived and Lizzie was the last of the bridesmaids to climb in. She looked back at the house where just her father and Rosie waited.

Rosie looked nervous, but lovely, and her father was still mouthing, "I do."

"Your turn next, Lizzie." Jessica, who was matron of honour, smiled.

"I'm never getting married," Lizzie declared.

"I used to say that when I was your age." Her sister laughed.

"You did?" Lizzie gasped. Surely Jessica had always been beautiful?

The trip to the church was short and soon over. Lizzie's mother was waiting for them and, as they got out of the car, she smoothed their dresses.

"I'll go and sit down," she said. "Rosie will be here any minute."

A small crowd had gathered outside the church. They looked at the other bridesmaids and said, "Ooooh," and, "Aaaah."

Lizzie dug her toe into the ground. She wished they wouldn't stare. They were probably thinking it was a shame there had to be an ugly one! She was just glad none of her friends had turned up — they'd have had a right old laugh!

Perhaps it would have been better if she'd broken her leg again, although that was not an experience she was keen to repeat.

In fact, since that accident, she'd kept out of trees, preferring to keep her feet firmly on the ground.

The other car pulled up and her father got out, then helped Rosie out.

"I do," he said.

Rosie smiled at them all, but her eyes lingered a little longer on Lizzie.

"You all look absolutely lovely," she said. "I'm proud of you."

Except me, Lizzie thought. I must look ridiculous.

"Is that you, Lizzie?" her father said. "Good lord! What a stunner!"

The church was packed with people. Lizzie held her head high and smiled nervously as she followed her sister down the aisle. She pretended she was beautiful, that people were looking at her and saying she looked lovely . . .

It was quite a fantasy, one she'd never indulged in before. Silence fell, apart from the shuffling of feet and the occasional cough.

"Who gives this woman?" the vicar asked.

"Me!" her father yelled, then groaned as a low rumble of laughter went round the congregation. Even Rosie giggled softly.

Lizzie's nervous smile grew and grew until she was grinning broadly. She wanted to burst out laughing, but knew she mustn't.

At last, the service was over and they went outside. Rosie was to have her photographs taken in the sun-drenched churchyard.

Lizzie was feeling quite cheerful until she saw the orchard — and the boys in the apple trees.

The boys. Her friends. Her gang . . .

She was mortified. If they saw her in this get-up, they'd never accept her as one of them again! She wanted to run and hide, but there was nowhere to go, no escape.

"Yoo hoo — Lizzie!"

She looked up and they all waved like mad. She waved back nervously.

Then it got worse. While the photographer ran around posing people for the pictures, the boys jumped out of the trees and ambled across the churchyard, hands in pockets, knees poking through their jeans.

Lizzie wished the ground would open beneath her feet.

"Wow!" Gary said, looking Lizzie up and down. "You don't half look pretty."

She felt heat rise in her cheeks. Pretty? And — was she blushing?

"You look like a princess," Sean added.

"You've got ever such a pretty face, Lizzie," Adam chipped in. "I'd never noticed it before."

The other boys all paid her similar compliments. They'd never said anything like that before, but then, they'd never seen her in a dress before with her hair all done and her face clean and with a touch of her sister's lipstick.

"You're good at climbing trees," or, "You're the best goalie we've ever had," were the usual compliments she attracted.

Well, they wouldn't want anything to do with her after this!

"Lizzie, come and have your photograph taken!" her mother called.

"I've got to go." She pulled a face, so they knew she'd rather be talking to them.

"See you later." Adam smiled. "You'll be coming tomorrow, won't you? We're going fishing."

She nodded. It hadn't made any difference to them!

As she hurried over to the others and joined the family group, she was smiling all over her face.

JUST before Rosie and Matt left the reception, to go on their honeymoon, everyone clustered outside. Rosie's unmarried friends waved their arms as she held her bouquet aloft.

"This way, Rosie!"

"Over here!"

"Me! Me!"

Rosie's eyes swept round and her gaze fell on Lizzie, standing at the back, still looking a bit lost and forlorn.

Growing up wasn't easy. It was a long and sometimes difficult journey, harder for some than for others.

"Here!" Rosie tossed the flowers into the air.

Lizzie looked up and saw them coming down towards her. She held out her hands and the flowers landed in them. She smiled as she buried her face in the soft blossom and drank in their delicious scent.

Maybe growing up wasn't going to be so bad after all. Like the spring breeze, it carried a promise of a summer of warmth and laughter. And the magical transformation of a child into a young woman . . . □

by BETTY PUTTICK

DOLLY dropped her shopping basket on the table with such a thump that her husband, Ted, lowered his newspaper to gaze at her.

"Something wrong, dear?" he asked mildly.

Dolly's round face was pink with annoyance.

"Lucy's having a birthday party," she announced. "And the whole of her class are invited. Twenty-two children!"

Ted smiled.

That's The Way To Do It!

"Don't tell me she's forgotten to invite you," he teased, but Dolly wasn't amused.

Ted decided a cup of tea was indicated. He knew Dolly wouldn't be able to keep it to herself, whatever was bothering her, and sure enough, as they sat drinking their tea, out it came.

Dolly had met her neighbour, Lucy, and her mother, down at the local shopping centre. With no children of their own, Ted and Dolly had become very fond of five-year-old Lucy, a lively, chatty little girl who often popped in to see them.

"Lucy ran up when she saw me," said Dolly. "She was so excited about the party. They've hired the church hall as there are so many children coming. 'You must come, Auntie Dolly,' she said. 'There are going to be clowns. Won't it be fun?' "

"So what's the problem, love?" Ted asked.

"It's Pat." Dolly frowned.

"As soon as Lucy mentioned it she didn't give me a chance to reply. 'Aunt Dolly wouldn't want to come, Lucy,' she said. I said if she needed any help I'd be glad to do anything I could, but she was quite offhand.

"Oh, Ted, she made me feel awful. I felt as if I was pushing myself in where I wasn't wanted."

Ted could see a suspicion of a tear in Dolly's eye.

"Come on, love," he said. "It's not the end of the world."

But he understood how Dolly felt.

Lucy's own grandparents were too far away to visit often, and Dolly liked to think that she had become an extra granny to the little girl. Apparently Lucy's mother didn't see her like that. But Dolly wasn't one to huff, and she got busy knitting a Fair Isle cardigan for Lucy's birthday present.

A COUPLE of days before the party, Lucy popped in after school looking rather upset.

"What's the matter, Lucy?" Dolly asked gently.

"It's the clowns." Lucy sniffed. "Mummy says they phoned to say they had made a mistake with the booking, and they can't come to my party after all."

"What a shame, dear!

"Has Mummy tried to get someone else?"

Lucy's lower lip trembled.

"Yes, she's tried everyone else she could think of, and they're all booked up. It won't be the same without the clowns, Auntie Dolly."

"Come on, Lucy, cheer up," said Ted. "Parties are always fun, and, who knows, there might be a surprise after all."

"Ted!" cried Dolly, after Lucy had gone. "Whatever made you say that to the child? Now she'll be expecting something and she'll be disappointed."

"Not if I have anything to do with it." He grinned. "You wanted to help with the party, and now you have the chance."

Ted smiled mysteriously and disappeared upstairs, while Dolly started cooking supper.

Later she called to tell him their meal was ready, but there was no reply. Whatever was he up to, she wondered?

"Ted," she called again, then almost dropped the plate she was holding as a strange little voice spoke.

"Hello, Dolly! Long time no see." A big red nose appeared round the door, followed by the unmistakable face of Mr Punch.

"Ted," said Dolly, "you can't."

"Why not? All kids love Punch and Judy. And, though I do say it myself, I'm not bad." He laid the puppet down by his plate.

"The puppets all look as good as new," he said, "and the frame is in the shed. I know where the curtains are. It would be great to do the old act again."

"But, Ted, these children are used to TV cartoons. Anyway, what would Pat say?"

"I'll soon find out." He grinned. "I'll pop round and see her later on, once Lucy's in bed."

He looked keenly at Dolly's doubtful face.

"She can only say no."

DOLLY smiled reminiscently as she remembered the day Ted had come home from a walk along the sea front to say that he'd just bought a Punch and Judy outfit!

He'd been just like a child — full of excitement.

He had been retired for nearly a year then, and Dolly knew he was bored. Their new little house by the sea had seemed such a good idea, but the house was in perfect order, and no DIY was required. And the garden was so small that there was very little work. He was obviously in need of a new interest.

On that particular day, Ted had stopped to talk to the Punch and Judy man.

"Don't think somehow I'll be back doing this job next year," he'd told Ted. "I'm not as fit as I once was. I don't suppose you'd know anyone who'd fancy taking over?"

So, much to his own surprise, Ted bought the outfit.

He learned how to put on a show and, in due course, he took the outfit down on to the sands.

He was a great success!

"You needn't think I'm going round with the collecting bag," Dolly teased.

"Not even for charity?" asked Ted artfully. "The hospital is saving up for a new scanner."

That summer, Dolly and Ted had attended many a charity fête with their Punch and Judy show.

That was almost two years ago now. Ted had not been well the following winter and somehow the Punch and Judy outfit had stayed packed away ever since.

Would he still be able to do it? When Ted returned from Pat's it was all fixed up.

"Pat welcomed me with open arms," he said.

"She said that she wanted to apologise for being so offhand the other day. She'd just spoken to the caterers and they'd been quibbling about numbers and the price. Lucy had been inviting everyone and they'd far more children than they could cater for . . .

"At least it's all sorted out now. It must be a lot of hard work to organise a party for five-year-olds!"

"Yes, I suppose so," Dolly agreed, nodding.

"Well, we'll be able to put on a good show for the kids, but we haven't got long to rehearse and I'm a bit rusty after all this time. I'll need you to help with the puppets so it all goes smoothly. I'm really looking forward to this."

DURING the next couple of days the little house echoed to cries of, "Where's the baby, Mr Punch?" and "That's the way to do it," as Punch despatched the other puppets one by one in his usual ruthless fashion.

They hired a couple of clown's costumes and, on the day of the party, Dolly was thankful for her wig of green curls and gaudy make-up as they helped to hide the fact that she was shaking inside!

Once they arrived at the church hall, there wasn't time to feel nervous. The children streamed in full of excitement, and before she knew it Dolly was playing the piano for Musical Bumps and the Birdie song, and Ted was in the middle of a balloon fight.

The children soon noticed the Punch and Judy stand in the corner.

"Punch and Judy! We want Punch and Judy!" they cried.

Ted disappeared behind the curtains and Dolly got the children sitting on the floor just as Mr Punch's familiar grinning face appeared over the top.

Afterwards, Dolly wondered what she'd been worried about. The old Punch and Judy routine worked its old magic, and the children laughed and shouted, loving every minute of it.

After tea, as the children were leaving, one by one they shouted goodbye to Mr Punch and Ted.

Lucy came up and slipped her hand into Dolly's.

"I'm glad the other clowns couldn't come, Auntie Dolly," she said. "It was the best party ever."

"I'll second that," Pat said, joining them. "Thank you so much, Dolly — and you, Ted."

Pat smiled as he approached, mopping his red face.

"Guess what?" he said. "Two of the mothers asked if I could take our Punch and Judy to their children's parties, too."

"And I suppose you said yes."

"I said I'd have to ask my partner." Ted grinned.

"Well, right now your partner would like a cup of tea and a nice long rest with her feet up," said Dolly, "but after that — who knows?"

Ted gave her a hug.

"That's the way to do it," he said. □

Close Encounter

ONE windless summer day
when the high peaks of Alligin
shimmered in dancing light,
and the blue sea-loch gleamed
through veils of mist below,
I left my pack and boots
and, for a while, walked barefoot,
soundlessly,
along the mossy ridge.
And so I came upon her unawares,
demure in velvet gown of smoky blue,
still as the stillness, silent as the stones.
In shared surprise,
we gazed upon each other guardedly,
she with limpid eyes
secret as peat-brown pools;
I, the stranger, trying to project
friendship, reassurance,
across the gulf of difference between
us.

Then, cautiously, I moved my
camera —
and, instantly estranged, she was
away,
a blue streak melting, merging
into the mottled mountain.
Belatedly regretting
the human need to capture and record
moments of fleeting beauty,
I stood, bereft, upon the empty ridge
watching the hills grow old in changing
light.
But something of the magic yet
remained,
so that I later wondered, secretly,
if I indeed encountered
a creature of the wild, that shining day
among the sun-warmed peaks of
Torridon —
or the Wise Woman of Beinn Alligin
in the guise of a mountain hare . . .

— Brenda G. Macrow.

A Change of Plan

by HELEN McKENZIE

THEY were fine girls and I was proud of them, the way they took life as it came, without complaint. Well, almost! Lorna'd found herself a Saturday job. It wasn't well paid, but it gave her just enough to buy those little things — hair ornaments, a trial make-up, magazines — so vital to survival at fourteen, which I simply couldn't afford.

I'd had to be much firmer, though, with Suzie when she pleaded for a paper round because I felt it'd be too dangerous. She had agreed reluctantly but still, she wasn't to be beaten.

I hadn't reckoned with the ingenuity of an eleven-year-old. She'd made some leaflets. laboriously printed out in her neatest hand, and circulated them among the neighbours. Offering her services. Any household tasks . . .

They'd laughed, but kindly, and they'd found some jobs for her. She swept up mowings from the lawn and polished cars for tired husbands, tidied kitchen cupboards for their weary wives, wound wool from skeins to balls for grandmothers. All in exchange for what she proudly pointed out was real money as she slid the clinking coins into her piggy-bank.

There wasn't anything I could do to comfort her.

"I wish we weren't so poor, Mum."

"We aren't," I answered firmly. "We may not have a lot of *things,* but we've got loads of love. That's rich like having money isn't."

Lorna gazed sadly at me.

"Sometimes I'd rather have a leather jacket," she said tearfully.

I was the really tearful one that night. It was the first time I'd cried in many years, for crying wouldn't bring my husband back. Tonight I saw him in my mind so clearly, the man the children couldn't quite recall, whose photo hung above the mantelpiece. David watching us, for ever young . . .

I wiped my eyes, abandoned hope of sleep and crept downstairs to warm some milk. He watched me from the photo. Him, for ever young, and me . . . I'd seen myself as I was passing in the mirror in the hall. Thirty-six and going on for fifty.

Those tears had done my face no favours, I reflected ruefully. Nor had the worried years alone with two small children to bring up and just a menial job as waitress in a local restaurant.

What I — what we all — needed was a break, a holiday. But holidays cost money that we didn't have.

Of course, we had our share of upsets. They wouldn't have been human if there hadn't been a time when Suzie mooched about for days because her best friend had a brand-new bike. I borrowed from the TV licence fund and bought one second hand. We painted it and it sufficed. But how I wished it could have been a spanking bright machine.

Poor Lorna, too, had her share of longing.

"Debby's got a brilliant leather jacket, Mum. All burgundy with fringing down the sleeves." She sighed. "It must have cost the earth."

I lit the gas beneath the milk pan and sat down wearily. Right then I would have settled for just one day off. But this was the holiday weekend and pretty well the busiest of the year.

STILL, we had our dreams and dreams were cheap enough. We used to watch the TV showing all the places people spent their holidays. From Brighton to Benares, Paris to Peru, we almost felt we'd been there, too.

It was a good attempt at self-deception and it worked, till now.

I was busy serving teas and chanced to overhear the chatter between two women, each wearing fancy hats.

"Of course," the navy pillbox said, nodding at a cream meringue, "now Simon's off to university, we're free to go a little out of season when it's cheaper."

"So sensible," the fawn straw murmured, pointing to a chocolate eclair.

"And so economical. My dear, we could do Madeira early and take a winter sunshine cruise."

I retreated. Economical, I thought, resentfully. Two holidays instead of one! Some people didn't know they were born! And there we were with nothing to look forward to, but praying for a spell of weather good enough to let us sunbathe in the garden.

Quite suddenly I couldn't take it any more. What did it matter if, just once, the bills were paid a little late? Besides, there was a little tucked away for rainy days. I stared out at the fine spring afternoon and momentarily the sun was lost behind an unexpected downpour . . .

I spent my coffee break collecting brochures from the travel agent and bore them home rejoicing.

The girls rejoiced as well.

"Don't raise your hopes too high," I warned. "We've left it very late. There may be nothing in our price range . . ."

"There's bound to be," Lorna declared with shining eyes.

I smiled forlornly. How the world looks golden to a child!

"Well, if there is, it won't be four-star luxury. We'll have to make the money stretch."

"We could go camping," Suzie said. "It would be ever so much fun to have a tent."

"I doubt it," I replied. "In my experience, tents are usually leaky efforts that collapse the moment you breathe."

"A caravan then," Lorna said.

"They're just as bad. Half-way to nowhere across muddy fields. No, I thought we might do slightly better. Go self-catering, of course, but in a cottage somewhere."

There were plenty to choose from in the brochures. We limited our choice to four sites not too far away because we'd have to travel by bus.

"Now all we've got to do is keep our fingers crossed we get a vacancy," I said. "I'll go tomorrow in my lunch hour."

I glanced at Suzie and her face was troubled.

"We'll need new clothes," she murmured.

"Oh no, we won't," Lorna put in before I could reply. "Ours may look old to us, but they'll be new to anyone we meet."

I almost laughed. The sheer logic of a teenage mind determined not to be deterred by trivialities!

They were up early for breakfast next day. Solemnly they handed me their money boxes.

"It's our contribution," Lorna said.

There was a tingling in my eyes and a lump in my throat. I shook my head.

"You ought to use that for some new clothes," I said. "You really do need T-shirts and some decent jeans."

I was completely lost for words that evening when they showed me what they'd bought. Three pairs of jeans and three shirts with matching logos. No fancy hat in town could hold a candle to the outfit my girls had bought me! I was so glad I could report that I'd had a tiny bit of luck, too. A chalet in a small park down in Kent was available.

"It only sleeps two, but they can fix up a camp bed for us. Not very comfy, but the best they could do. We only had the chance of this one as the couple who were going to have it cancelled yesterday."

The girls were whooping round the kitchen with delight. The thought of cramming three into a space designed for two was nothing in their eyes, although it worried me a bit. Still, we'd be out all day and, after all, it had been so much cheaper than the others. I glanced at David's photo and smiled a little sadly.

"You should have stayed," I whispered. "Nobody ever thinks of catering for threes. It's such a rotten number when you could and should be four."

IT was a glorious afternoon when we arrived. The chalets were spread out across the fields among the trees and bathed in dappled sunlight. An idyllic spot, I told myself, worth every penny. This would be a fortnight to remember.

The centre of the operation was a gorgeous Tudor manor, hardly modified as far as I could see except for the addition of an oak reception desk. We waited there for ages, but nobody came. Eventually I rang the bell.

Far down the hall, a door swung open and a man appeared. Tall, fortyish, with horn-rimmed glasses just like David used to wear. He gazed at us. I waited for him to approach, but he didn't.

He just stood there awkwardly. And then I saw and understood. Two tiny fists were clutching at his trousers from behind. A boy's face peered round at us and stuck a tongue out. The girls went pink with pent-up laughter.

"Mr Walters?" I inquired.

He nodded.

"Excuse me just one moment, please," he said and bent to extricate himself.

"My sister Joanne's," he said, as he swung the child up in his arms. "He's got this knack of catching me so I can't move. It's quite embarrassing at times."

I smiled, remembering the tricks my two had played when they were small.

"Don't worry," I said, "we're in no hurry. Merely checking in. Chalet Fourteen. Mrs Hicks."

He set the child down on the counter and ran his finger down the list of names. And then he glanced at me and ran his fingers through his hair distractedly.

"Is something wrong?" I asked a little anxiously.

He reddened.

"I'm afraid there's some mistake. A double booking. Chalet Fourteen's taken. Third time this month," he muttered. "Never happened till Joanne insisted we computerise the system."

"But you've another?"

He shook his head.

"We're absolutely full. I could offer you September."

Before I could say anything, poor Suzie's face had crumpled and

HIDDEN VILLAGES OF SCOTLAND

AUCHMITHIE

FOR centuries the fisherfolk of Auchmithie, on the rugged coast of Angus, formed a community very much their own. They were closely connected with the sea, with a bit of crofting as a sideline.

The village was very isolated, but being fairly self-supporting, the folk disliked outside interference. Strangers were eyed with suspicion, tax collectors were stoned from the village!

Auchmithie was the original home of the smoked haddock, or "smokie", and it was only when families began to migrate to Arbroath's better harbour and facilities that the name "Arbroath Smokies" became widely known.

The picturesque site of the village now makes it a great tourist attraction, but even in the 18th century Sir Walter Scott made use of it as the fictional "Musselcrag" in his novel, "The Antiquary".

Over fifty years ago I can remember an early film being shot here. It was called "Christie Johnstone", and featured that romantic star of the early days, Stewart Rome. Handsome, elegant and ever polite — only "grannies" will remember him striding across Auchmithie's storm beaches in those far-off days.

her eyes had filled with tears.

"We can't afford the bus fare twice," she blurted out.

I felt myself go scarlet under Mr Walters' gaze.

"It would be difficult," I murmured. "School time . . ."

"Perhaps you'd like to talk about it over tea," he said. "You've had a long trip and besides I'd be so glad of adult company. Our Danny's very good but, well, he can be trying when his mum's away on these computer courses. Besides, the separation must be hurting."

"Separation?"

"Joanne and Mike, her husband. That's why she's back here bothering me," he added wryly.

"I'm sorry."

"Don't be. For me, maybe — I managed better on my own — but not for them. I reckon this'll be the making of them. Mike's started phoning every day and as for dear Joanne, well, you can see from what she's done with Chalet Fourteen where her mind is! Now what about that tea?"

THE girls adored the chance to mother Danny. They fed him ice-cream and then took him on the lawn outside to play while Mr Walters sat indoors with me. A pretty girl brought tea and home-made cake. It was a luxury indeed to have someone to wait on me and made me realise how desperately I needed this holiday. The two weeks it seemed I wouldn't get.

I think it must have shown in my face, despite the efforts that I made to keep a cheerful front for Mr Walters, having offered me a refund, suddenly fell silent.

"It isn't good enough," he murmured to himself. "Not good enough at all. Computers! Sisters! Oh no! Not nearly good enough."

I sipped my tea and watched the girls with Danny. I hadn't seen the pair of them so happy for such a long time. My heart ached with the knowledge I was going to have to take them home that evening.

"I know it's not the same, not what you wanted," Mr Walters said, emerging from his thoughts, "but would you possibly consider an alternative?"

"Would I?"

"We've several bedrooms free in the west wing. Not quite as private as the chalets, but they have a bathroom. And there would be meals from our kitchen if you wouldn't mind too much eating with the family. There's just Joanne and me. And," he added with an apologetic smile, "Danny."

"It's very kind," I murmured, "but we couldn't."

"It wouldn't be so very bad," he said persuasively. "For a small boy, he can be quite angelic sometimes. But I suppose you're right. It isn't what you wanted . . ."

His voice trailed sadly into silence.

"Oh no!" I put in hastily. "It isn't that. It would be heavenly. You've no idea. But, well, to put it bluntly, I simply couldn't find the extra cost."

Dragonfly Destination

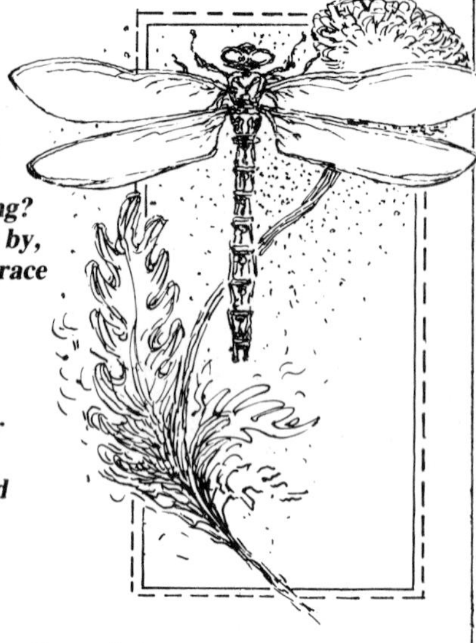

***O**H, where do you travel, you*
gossamer thing,
Excitedly whirring on delicate wing?
Whenever I see you alight or pass by,
I'm dazed by your beauty, your grace
as you fly.

Your aerodynamics and aircraft
design,
And gauzy, lace wings which your
body align,
Are taking you over the hedge and
away.
Oh, where do you travel on this
summer's day.?

— Chrissy Greenslade.

"Extra? There'd be no extra!" he exclaimed. "It's our fault entirely."

I smiled.

"In that case, I can't think of anything we would like better."

He glanced outside and grinned.

"Looks very much like Danny feels the same. He's having some terrific fun with your two girls."

He shook my hand that evening as we said goodnight. The gentle pressure wakened something in me that I'd thought would never stir again.

I WON'T forget that holiday. How could I? It's changed all of our lives. I've spent the winter evenings studying a course in leisure management. In the spring I shall hand my apron in and leave the café. I'll be working with Richard Walters from now on. The girls will be transferring to a school in Kent.

Yes, it's worked out very well. Joanne is going home to Mike, relieved that I can manage the computer better than she ever did. I didn't think I would, but now I understand it, I'm quite smitten. It wasn't the same kind of whirlwind romance that I found with Richard, but, then, you never have two love affairs that are the same.

I've seen that message many times this winter shining in my David's eyes and I know he's happy for me. Almost as happy as I am myself. □

Bossy By Name

by PEGGY MORRIS

"WHY Bossyboots?" Sheila Holden asked incredulously as she cuddled the puppy her neighbour had just brought home from the kennels.

"For heaven's sake, Jan, he's got a pedigree as long as your arm, and a proper kennel name. You could surely have thought of a more appropriate name for him."

Jan Munro laughed.

"If you'd seen him in the pen with his mother and the other puppies, you'd realise why. He was organising everyone, even his mother!"

She took the puppy from her neighbour, putting her face down to his.

"You and I," she told him, "are going to get along just fine. Welcome to your new home, Bossyboots."

Bossyboots responded by licking her nose enthusiastically.

Sheila got up from her chair.

"I'd best be getting home. I was in the middle of tidying David's bedroom when I looked out of the window and saw you were back from the kennels.

"I suppose I'd better go and finish what I started."

Jan walked to the door with her, still holding Bossyboots.

"I must say," Sheila said, "he's not behaving like most puppies just taken from their mothers into a new and strange environment. He hasn't cried once and looks quite at home. What have you got there, Jan — the makings of a superdog?"

"I hope so." Jan pushed her hair back from her eyes. "By the way, I've decided not to call him Bossyboots, it's too long."

"Good," Sheila replied. "So what are you going for instead?"

"Bossy, I think — short for Bossyboots!"

SHEILA was away down the path and into her own drive as Jan shut the door and turned back into the small, comfortable home she had shared with her father until a few weeks ago.

The last seven years hadn't been easy. First, she'd been nursing her mother, who had died three years ago, and afterwards her father, who had never really recovered from her mother's death.

She had been alone now in the small house for six weeks, and knew already that she wasn't going to enjoy it much.

Hence the arrival of Bossy. He would be company, an excuse to hear her own voice, a reason for getting up in the morning and the object of affection she needed.

Bossy finished sniffing round the kitchen and came to sit at her feet. He stretched himself upwards on his hind legs, and kneaded his front paws on her skirt. He gave a sharp, short, demanding little bark.

Jan bent and lifted him on to her lap.

"OK," she said resignedly. "I heard you."

Content now, Bossy curled himself around on her lap and immediately fell fast asleep. Jan stroked his silky coat and went back to her thoughts.

For all the loneliness she felt, she knew she was lucky. The house was entirely hers and her father had left her a comfortable income in his will. At thirty, she at least had no financial worries.

But sometimes she envied Sheila for her happy family life with her husband and young son.

During the next few weeks Jan concentrated on training her little dog. At first he rebelled against the lead, digging his heels in and refusing to move with the gentle pull she gave it.

But soon he realised that to obey Jan meant a walk down by the canal.

Sleeping in the kitchen wasn't received well at first either. For several nights his howls echoed through the house, until Jan began to wonder if she would have to give in and bring his basket into her room.

But on the fifth night silence reigned, and in the morning he greeted her with his usual delight.

It wasn't until she looked into his basket that she realised why last night had been different.

There, in the corner of his basket, was the teddy-bear which usually sat in the chair in her bedroom. Bossy must have got into her room and dragged Ted out.

She looked at Bossy, who was watching her, eagle-eyed, his tail wagging furiously.

"Well, if he helps you sleep you can keep him," she said, and put Ted back in the corner of Bossy's basket.

It was becoming very clear that Bossy was no ordinary dog. He was a thinker, an organiser, a dog who knew when to give in and when to get his own way.

LATER that day Jan and Bossy were in the garden — Bossy chasing flies to his heart's content.

"Hi, Jan. How are you getting on?" Sheila leaned over the fence.

"Just fine. He's so full of energy," Jan said, smiling.

"You know," Sheila said, watching him, "I'm not sure that you've done the right thing by bringing Bossy into your life."

"Why not?" Jan protested, bending to stroke him. "He's company for me."

Sheila looked at her sympathetically.

"But you're young, Jan, you shouldn't be living this way. You ought to be out and about, meeting people — maybe having a job. But now you've taken on another responsibility which means you can't do any of that."

"There are other people who need jobs more than me, Sheila. It would seem a bit silly.

"As for meeting people — " Jan gave an embarrassed little laugh. "It's years since I had freedom. It takes time, Sheila, to get back into that."

Three weeks later Bossy was coming on by leaps and bounds. She began teaching him to come to heel and stay until called.

"You really are a clever little dog," she told him at the end of another three weeks, preparing to take him for a walk along the towpath. "I don't think we need the lead today, and this road's very quiet."

Everything went well until they reached the corner of the road, with the canal in sight. Suddenly Bossy darted across the road to greet a spaniel he'd spotted.

There was a sudden shriek of brakes as a car swerved to avoid Bossy, who reached the other side safely and was sniffing noses with the spaniel completely unaware of the chaos he had just caused.

The car stopped and the driver got out. He crossed to where Jan was standing as though turned to stone.

"Do you realise you could have caused a very serious accident?" he shouted. "A young dog like that needs discipline and training. Take him to obedience classes, keep him on a lead. Do anything except allow him to wander all over the road!"

"I'm sorry." Jan at last found her voice. "I have been training him.

He's very intelligent, he learns quickly, I really thought he was all right walking to heel — "

"He's too young to understand properly." He spoke with an authority that sent a shudder through Jan.

But before she could say anything more, Bossy had run across the road again and was standing between them, tail wagging, eyes bright.

"You see?" The dark-haired man threw up his hands. "He's done it again. For goodness' sake, put him on the lead before he causes any more trouble!"

He turned on his heel, returned to his car and drove off without another glance in their direction. The spaniel's owner gave Jan a disapproving look before going on his way.

SEVERAL things occupied Jan over the next few weeks. One of them was Bossy's training and he seemed to be back on track again, though sometimes she thought he was only doing it to keep in her good books.

Then there was the argument she'd had with the man she and Bossy had upset. She'd felt patronised by him and it had made her feel older and dowdier than her thirty years.

She found herself studying her reflection in the mirror, piling her hair in a knot on the top of her head to give her a more sophisticated air. But she always let it fall again.

Last of all, it was the thought of the man himself. Dark-haired, dark-eyed, tall and slim, he was there in her mind and would not go away. Even the thought that he might be married didn't put her off.

It was a long time since she'd thought of anyone in that way. There had been boyfriends, but at the time she'd been too young to get serious.

Then, when she'd had to give up her job to look after her parents, she'd resigned herself to the fact that she might well remain single.

The day Bossy fell sick was a hot one, with a hint of thunder in the air.

He seemed fine in the morning, while Jan was having her breakfast.

He then spent half an hour at the bottom of the garden, rooting around in the weeds that crept through the fence from the field beyond. Then he came in, settled in his basket, and went to sleep.

At one o'clock he was still there. At two o' clock he stirred slightly when Jan stroked him, but didn't move any further. Half an hour later he staggered out into the garden, looking extremely unwell. Jan immediately called to Sheila over the fence and then carried him indoors.

When Sheila arrived Jan was already on the phone to the vet.

"He'll be here in five minutes. Thanks for coming over, Sheila," Jan said.

"No problem. I'm sure he'll be fine." Sheila patted the limp dog gently. "Would you mind if I went? I have to pick up David from school."

"No, you go ahead," Jan said. "We'll be fine."

When Sheila had gone Jan sat beside the table, stroking Bossy's coat and talking gently to him. A few minutes later someone came around the side of the house and in through the kitchen door.

"So this is where the sick dog is," said a deep, attractive voice. "You did tell me to come in this way. You must be Miss Munro — "

The words trailed away as she turned to face him. Dark-haired, dark-eyed, tall and slim, he was all too familiar to Jan. They stared at each other in dawning recognition.

"So we meet again." The vet shook her hand. "Steve Wilson." He moved to the table and bent over Bossy. "How long has he been like this?"

Jan explained what had happened that morning, and looked worriedly at Bossy.

"I would imagine he ate something that didn't agree with him. A common complaint with dogs. I'll give him something to settle his stomach and see how it goes."

It went like magic. In five minutes, Bossy was starting to look himself again. Steve Wilson stroked him, and gave him one last check.

He lifted Bossy from the table and put him down in his basket with Ted. "He'll be all right now. But call me again if you're worried. My receptionist left to have a baby, so watch out for the answer phone."

"And are you coping?" Jan asked. "Without any help, I mean?"

"Just. It does make things a bit difficult — managing by yourself."

They paused on the path outside the kitchen, their backs to the door.

"Look, I want to apologise for the way I spoke to you the last time we met. I was in a rush and I was probably going too fast. I don't even know your dog's name." He smiled as Bossy made his way unsteadily into the garden.

"It's Bossy."

"Bossy?" He looked incredulous.

"Short for Bossyboots. Because that's what he is. He'll organise everybody and anything if he's given a chance. In the nicest possible way, of course." She smiled.

"And I accept your apology. For Bossyboots as well as for myself. And if you need a receptionist, what about me? I'm not too bothered about the money, as long as I can bring Bossyboots with me."

Steve laughed.

"Of course," he said. "I wouldn't have it otherwise. After all, he made it possible for me to apologise and put things right between us."

He bent down and patted the little dog who immediately tried to clamber into his arms.

"And he also likes to be the centre of attention."

Bossy sat between them, looking from one to the other. He felt very content with the way things were turning out.

He had always wanted to be part of a family. □

Young At Heart

NANCY let herself in through the kitchen door, shook her umbrella out, and hung up her dripping mac. What a day for the start to her holiday!

Her final chores done, now she simply had to wait until her son-in-law came to pick her up.

Unable to settle to anything, she checked over her suitcase once more. She smiled as she thought of the new lacy nightie and negligée that she'd bought especially for this holiday.

In all their years of travelling to sunnier climes, she and Don had always treated themselves to a few new things. The nightie and negligée were her little treat to herself this summer.

If Don had been here, he'd have been amused at her choice. The pale pink

by CATRIONA FYFE

ruffles, the lace edging, the satin trim all seemed quite frivolous. Their daughter, Doreen, would doubtless make some disparaging comment about her age, but who cared?

Snapping the case shut, she carried it through to the lobby, then went back to stand at the kitchen window.

She wondered if it would be raining as hard when they reached Broadstairs.

That was the one thing about British holidays — you couldn't be sure of the weather. She and Don had preferred to take off-season breaks abroad.

As the doorbell heralded Alan's arrival, she was brought back to the present with a jolt. Don had been dead for almost two years now. Nancy hadn't been able to bring herself to book a solo holiday, so Doreen had stepped in.

"You need a break, Mum," Doreen had said firmly. "Do your own thing next year, if you like — but this summer you're holidaying with us!"

Nancy opened the door to find her son-in-law, Alan, and her granddaughter, Rona, standing dripping on the doorstep.

"Ready, Mum?" Alan smiled. "You *have* packed a dressing-gown, haven't you? You'll need it if the weather stays like this."

Nancy nodded brightly.

"It's all taken care of," she assured him, trying not to smile at the thought of her new negligée.

"And a hot water — " Rona began.

"I do *not* need a hot-water bottle," Nancy reproved her indignantly.

"Don't be so touchy, Gran — I was going to say, have you got a waterproof?"

Nancy accepted the rebuke with good humour.

"Yes, I'm taking my mac."

"Right, let's go, then." Alan grinned. "Shall I lock up?"

"Leave it to me," Nancy said firmly.

Honestly, anyone would think she was an old lady, not the sprightly seventy-year-old she knew herself to be!

It rained all the way to Kent and the heavy skies showed no sign of clearing as they eventually pulled up outside the hotel.

A pleasant-faced young man helped Alan and Rona carry the cases upstairs while Doreen and Nancy signed the visitors' book.

They soon joined Alan who was busily unpacking his and Doreen's case.

Rona and Nancy were sharing a room and the young girl brought extra cups through to her parents' room, to make tea.

"Well, we've landed on our feet this time," Doreen commented. "Everything seems very comfortable, and the receptionist is charming."

Alan cast his daughter a sharp look, and nodded knowingly.

"To judge by the way Rona's eyes lit up, so is the lad who carried our cases. He's probably one of the waiters. Handsome enough, I dare say — if a bit skinny!"

"Honestly, Dad! I hardly noticed him!" Rona flushed.

After their tea, Rona helped Nancy unpack. Knowing that her new nightie and negligée were near the bottom of the case, Nancy waited to see how Rona would react.

The teenager's whistle of admiration was as gratifying as it was unexpected.

"Hey, Gran — that's lovely! Puts my nightshirt to shame!"

Then there was a tap at the door.

"Are you two ready to come down now?" Doreen called. "We don't want to miss lunch."

Rona opened the door.

"Yes — just coming."

Nancy grabbed her hairbrush.

"Leave me the key, Rona — I'll follow you down."

AFTER hastily tidying her hair and applying a touch of lipstick, Nancy went downstairs. She found the rest of the family already seated round a table, chatting to a man who was possibly five or ten years her senior.

" . . . and give her a bit of a break," she overheard Doreen say. "She was widowed a couple of years ago . . . still hasn't really got over it."

Nancy felt the blood rush to her cheeks.

What a nerve — telling a complete stranger all about me, she fumed. Doreen could be so tactless!

Jingling her keys loudly, she entered the room, managing to force a bright smile.

"Here I am at last," she said. "Have you ordered yet?"

"Try the steak and kidney pie," the stranger volunteered. "I always do. And Madge's trifle is out of this world."

Nancy nodded primly as she glanced down the menu.

'Thanks — I might take your advice. What about the rest of you?"

She hadn't meant to sound cold, but the man must have heard the edge in her voice. Turning away slightly, he opened a magazine.

Once they'd eaten, Alan pushed his chair back contentedly.

"After a dinner like that, I could just enjoy a little snooze . . . "

"Oh, Dad!" Rona protested.

I'll show them, Nancy decided.

"Don't worry, Rona — I'm still game for a walk, if you are."

First Love

ONCE upon a lifetime
Comes a splendoured thing;
Mightier than a mistral —
Younger than the spring.
Through the commonplace it weaves
A shining thread of gold.
Not what you have dreamed of —
Not what you were told.
Each moment is enchanted,
The whole wide world is new,
And all the birds are bluebirds
When first love comes to you.

— Gaye Wilson.

The man lowered his magazine and smiled at them, more cautiously this time.

"You could go to Bleak House. Then, if you're feeling really sprightly, there's a lighthouse farther along. It's a nice walk."

Nancy glanced defiantly at her son-in-law.

"Well, that'll blow the cobwebs away. Come on, Rona — we'll get our coats."

There was still a light drizzle in the air, but they pushed on gamely. The wind was blowing into their faces and when they reached a wooden bus shelter, Nancy pulled her granddaughter into the landward side and paused, gasping for breath.

"I give up," she panted. "Let's get the bus back."

Rona nodded ruefully.

"Sorry I dragged you out, Gran — Mum'll kill me when she sees the state of us."

"Rubbish!" Nancy snorted. "I'm as much to blame. I wish I could convince your mother that I'm not a helpless old wreck yet!"

"She means well, Gran," Rona said earnestly. "Is that — is that why you didn't really want to come on holiday with us?"

Nancy looked at her granddaughter guiltily. Had it been so obvious?

"I just don't want to be a nuisance . . . "

ALTHOUGH neither suffered any ill effects from their outing, Rona and Nancy were glad to fall in with Doreen's plans for the following day. They all enjoyed the coach trip she'd suggested. And, once they got back to the hotel, Alan made a surprise announcement.

"I'm taking my wife out for a special meal tonight," he said, with a smile. "We never had a chance to celebrate our anniversary last week so this is it! You won't feel too neglected?"

"Oh, we'll be fine," Nancy assured him.

"And you'll keep an eye on Rona?" Doreen asked her mother.

"Honestly, Mum — I'm sixteen. Gran doesn't need to act as babysitter!" Rona groaned.

"Well, no . . . " Doreen demurred. "But — "

"But nothing," Nancy declared briskly. "You just go off and have a good time — you deserve it. We'll both be fine."

Their own dinner over, Rona stuffed her bikini and a towel into a carrier-bag, while Nancy settled down in an easy chair and switched the television on.

"What time shall I expect you back, Rona?"

"Oh, I won't be late. I'm going for a quick swim while it's warm enough. Since the weather's brightened up a bit, I may as well make the most of it.

"And Charlie — that young waiter who works here — asked if I'd like to go for a coffee later on. That's OK, isn't it?"

Barely waiting for Nancy's good-humoured nod, Rona waved cheerily and dashed out.

HIDDEN VILLAGES OF SCOTLAND

KIRKINCH (near Meigle, Perthsire)

KIRKINCH lies in the Perthshire lowlands not far from Meigle — yet in a world of its own, well away from busy traffic routes.

Quiet and sheltered, it has an air of contentment. In early summer many of the cottages are half-buried in apple and pear-tree blossom. The ruined church on the knoll gives the village its name. An "inch" is an island, and this knoll formerly stood up like one in an area of fields and pastures too apt to be flooded.

One autumn of bad harvesting weather in the 17th century, the minister of his dutiful flock advised them to forget it was the Sabbath and to make full use of the first bright, dry day for weeks.

Just as he said that, there was a tremendous crash and the roof fell in! The congregation took it to mean the wrath of God, fled the building and never went back. The kirk was never rebuilt.

Kirkinch folk are long-lived, and praise the water of the local "Cally Well." At one time every cottage had its water-barrel collecting rain-water from the roof, and a garden draw-well. Plenty of water — a saleable commodity, these days in the 1990s.

Perhaps it's better to avoid contact with commercial enterprise, and to sit back and enjoy the peaceful atmosphere and the scent of blossom.

Nancy picked up her newspaper and flicked through to the television pages. There was nothing she felt like watching.

Maybe she ought to go out, too. But where? She searched through the paper again. Was there a cinema, maybe? Or a playhouse?

Suddenly a large, boxed advertisement caught her eye. A brass band at the pavilion! Yes, that was just what she fancied — and she still had half an hour before it started.

Impulsively, she pulled her favourite red dress out of the wardrobe and changed hastily.

She handed in her keys and left a message for Rona at the reception desk, then hurried down the street. It might not be a great adventure, she told herself, but I'm proving I can still think for myself!

AS she sank into her seat, the band was just tuning up. Then they began to play a brisk march which soon had Nancy's foot tapping in time.

For over an hour she sat enthralled, as they played a medley of waltzes and quicksteps, military-sounding marches and light-hearted popular melodies.

The audience responded warmly, and Nancy enthusiastically joined in the applause at the end. It had been so enjoyable that she didn't really want to go straight back to the hotel, yet she felt she couldn't very well go for a coffee on her own. Sighing, Nancy thought she should get back and clambered into a waiting taxi.

"Where to, love?"

Nancy leaned forward.

"I'm staying at the . . . the Sea . . . " She scratched her head impatiently. How could she have forgotten? "I'm sorry — I know it's the Sea something-or-other. Oh, this is so silly!"

"Sea View?" he prompted. "Sea Haven? Or was it the Seacrest Lodge?"

"No — it's none of those. I'm with my family, you see. They did the booking. No excuse, I know, but . . . "

"Why don't I take another fare, then come back for you? Then you might remember," the driver suggested sympathetically.

"I could try."

Fancy getting in a mess like this! Nancy felt angry with herself as she climbed out of the taxi and made for a nearby bench.

The bench creaked as someone sat down at the opposite end, but she didn't look up. Preoccupied, she shook her head as she began sorting through her handbag, hoping against hope that something in it might jog her memory.

"You can't have lost your keys," came a familiar-sounding voice. "I saw you hand them in."

SHE didn't recognise him at first. He was wearing a blue and white windcheater and an improbably youthful baseball cap. But then he turned to face her and she recognised the cheery grin of the man from the hotel.

Nancy felt colour rise in her cheeks.

"You'll hardly believe this," she said after a pause. "I've forgotten the name of the hotel." She glanced down at her lap, expecting him to laugh, but his voice was level when he spoke.

"Yes, I can see that could pose a problem," he agreed. "It's the Seagulls' Nest." He was smiling gently when Nancy looked up into his face, and she couldn't help responding.

"Look, I was just going across the road to that ice-cream bar for a knickerbocker glory. Why don't you join me? Then I'll escort you back."

"Oh, I wouldn't want to impose . . . "

He stood up, holding his arm out in a courtly gesture.

"You'd be doing *me* the favour, my dear. I don't much like sitting on my own when the rest of the world is in pairs."

She smiled nervously but evaded his arm.

"The would be very nice," she said quietly. "Now I'd better introduce myself — I'm Nancy —"

"Nancy Campbell, if my memory serves me right?"

"How did you — ?"

He laughed.

"I saw your name on the bookings sheet. I'm the father of the present proprietor and ran the hotel before Fred and his wife,

Madge, took over. I can't help still taking an interest.

"Bert Simms is my name."

As they reached the ice-cream parlour, he held the door open for Nancy.

"Where shall we sit? By the window?"

"That'd be fine by me." She nodded. Nancy gazed out of the window, watching a steady stream of holidaymakers strolling homewards. She smiled as a young couple walked out of the evening gloom towards the ice-cream parlour, hand-in-hand.

"Young love." She sighed wistfully, turning to smile gently at Bert. "Those were the days . . . "

Bert glanced outside and chuckled softly.

"They were indeed. But that's your granddaughter and *my* grandson! Oh, poor Charlie — he'll die of embarrassment if he sees me."

Peeping over a strategically-held menu, Nancy recognised the young waiter from the hotel. He was wearing a handsome bandsman's uniform and had an instrument case tucked under his arm.

"A man of many talents?" she murmured.

Bert nodded proudly.

"Yes, he's very musical. He's hoping to go to music college, but he's just working for his mum during the holidays at the moment."

As they covertly watched Rona and Charlie, Nancy suddenly began to laugh.

"Something I said?" Bert asked, puzzled.

"Oh, no — it's just — well, my daughter has been fussing and fretting over me so much. And I was supposed to be keeping an eye on Rona this evening . . . "

Bert laughed with her.

"Come along." He grinned. "Let's finish our ices and get out of here before people start staring at us — and before we're noticed by those two love-birds over there!"

They hurried out, still giggling.

"Just think," Bert said, "your daughter wouldn't have let either of you out of her sight if she knew what you'd get up to when you were off the leash . . ."

As he offered his arm again, Nancy clutched at it gratefully. It was a rather nice feeling, she reflected wonderingly.

She looked up at him.

"Off the leash," she murmured. "Yes, that's just how it feels. Grown-up children can be so over-protective, can't they?"

"They mean well," Bert commented, unconsciously echoing Rona's words of the previous evening. "But now you're out, let's live dangerously.

"There's a bigger hotel along the front, which has a very nice cocktail bar. Would you like to accompany me?" he asked formally.

I'm glad I changed my dress, Nancy thought contentedly.

"Thank you — I'd like that very much," she told him with a smile. "Very much indeed." □

I LOOKED up as the office door opened, and smiled when Sam Carter walked in.

I had begun work for the firm of accountants in February. It was now April and I'd seen Sam nearly every week.

He worked for Ibbotson's, a small but profitable business which rented out farm equipment. Our firm had been handling Ibbotson's finances for years.

"Everything ready for me, Lucy?" Sam smiled hopefully.

"Sorry." I shook my head. "The farmer who was supposed to return your tractor to the depot yesterday hasn't. And

he's quibbling about the charges —"

"Oh no! But they shouldn't expect you to deal with that — I'll see what I can sort out."

"Actually, Mr Smythe is trying to contact them now. How about some coffee while you wait?"

He nodded, still frowning.

When I returned to the office with the coffee, the telephone shrilled.

Sam took his coffee and walked over to the window gazing out at the old grey walls of Skipton Castle.

As I replaced the receiver, he turned, leaning against the window-ledge.

"At least we both chose lovely surroundings to lick our wounds," he said quietly.

I looked at him, startled. He had told me he'd moved to Yorkshire after a rather painful divorce, but I had never told him my own reasons for moving to Skipton. How did he know about Nigel . . ?

As I hesitated, Ron Smythe, my boss, came in.

"Sorry, Sam, but we haven't been able to get in touch with the farmer yet. He's still out in the fields, but should be back any time." He frowned.

"Look, how about you and Lucy slipping out for a pub lunch —"

"Oh, but I've heaps to do," I interrupted quickly.

"Nothing that can't wait," Ron Smythe assured me. "Put it on expenses."

Ibbotson's were one of our best customers, so I couldn't argue.

Half an hour later we were sitting in the beautiful old lounge bar at a local hotel, with a ploughman's lunch and a shandy in front of us.

Any hope I had that Sam might have forgotten his surprising remark was soon shattered.

"It's all right, Lucy. I'm not prying, but I know you've been unlucky in love, too. You seemed to understand so much when I told you about my divorce."

I cut my cheese and looked down at my plate as I answered.

"Well, it's all over now . . . I was about to be married but it was all called off at the last minute."

In spite of myself, I shuddered at the painful memories.

"Nigel met someone else." My words seemed to hang in

the air and I struggled to keep my voice light. "I couldn't stay in Bournemouth after everything that had happened there . . ."

He nodded.

"I can understand that. At least I didn't run quite as far as you. Only from Sheffield."

THERE was a brief silence as we ate, then he spoke again.

"I was always fond of the Yorkshire Dales, but it's only since I moved here that I've begun to appreciate their true beauty. The vast fells, the open space, the thrill of mastering the heights, all bring a sense of peace. I discovered tranquillity." He was smiling as he spoke.

"Well, I haven't really seen much of the Dales. I've had so much to do . . ."

"But you can't live in the gateway to the Dales and not enjoy them."

"I've driven through —" I said, slightly on the defensive, but he only smiled.

"There's only one way to see the Dales and that's on foot. I go every weekend," he told me, his voice slightly wistful.

"Are you one of those hardy souls who hikes around in big boots with a huge pack on your back?" I grinned, but he shook his head.

"I'm no mountaineer."

"Well, walking has never been *my* strong point," I admitted. "I suppose I've never made the time . . ."

He looked at me thoughtfully before he spoke.

"Look, Lucy, I've walked all through the winter on my own. I know you don't want to get involved, after Nigel, but I'm just looking for a walking companion. I'm sure I'd enjoy exploring the countryside with you. I'd like to share the beauty, the peace . . ."

His dark grey eyes were sincere and I couldn't help thinking how different he was from Nigel.

"I don't know . . ." Perhaps it was still too soon.

"You can't live in the past for ever," he said gently. "Look, I'll be in Grassington carpark next Saturday. It's easy to find. We can just walk by the river, have an easy day to begin with, a pub lunch — then if you've had enough —" He shrugged.

I didn't answer, I didn't know what to say. We drained our glasses and stood up.

"I'll wait there until eleven o'clock. I'd like you to come," he added.

When we got back to the office, everything was sorted out. He didn't mention his invitation again.

As I cleared my desk, and made my way to the small, comfortable flat that had become my haven, I told myself I wouldn't go. I'd long since decided my career was going to be all that mattered. Never again would I risk the pain of rejection.

The April sun lit my flat and from my window I could look down at the tourists. They all seemed to be in couples.

"I'm just looking for a walking companion," he had assured me.

Just one day, I decided, wouldn't do any harm.

He was there before me, leaning on the back of his car, drinking coffee.

He showed no surprise when I drew up beside him. He gave his lazy smile and poured me a cup of coffee.

"The best way to start a walk," he assured me.

I stood enjoying my coffee in the warm, April sun feeling suddenly at ease. Then we were ready to go.

That walk was the first of many.

THE months seemed to slip by and soon it was September.

I drove along the narrow, stone-walled lanes of the Dales to our meeting point.

I had long since learned to find the locations Sam marked on my Ordnance Survey Map. I had long since progressed from trainers to walking shoes, then to boots. I had waterproofs and a haversack, and I loved the Dales.

Why then, for the first time since our meeting in Grassington, was I feeling apprehensive about the day?

During the summer Sam had become my best friend. We had talked about his divorce, and my unhappy split from Nigel.

We had walked for hours. Gradually I managed longer distances, climbed higher, learned to ignore the rain, even to enjoy it.

We had talked about our work, music, books — sometimes shared a meal after the walk was over, but more often going our separate ways. And it had been just as Sam had said — friendship and companionship.

Sam was promoted and no longer came to my office, his place taken by a middle-aged lady.

Sometimes I wished I had never met Sam — he had changed my life. But even as the thought crossed my mind, I knew I wouldn't have missed the last few months together for anything.

Perhaps it was only my imagination that things had changed between us over the last few weekends. But there was nothing I could put my finger on. Sometimes I saw an unfamiliar expression in his grey eyes; a tender note in his voice . . .

As usual, Sam was waiting for me.

I looked round when I climbed out of my car and saw a range of hills, higher and steeper than anything I had attempted before. I gasped and Sam laughed at my shocked expression.

"Don't worry, our path is over there." He nodded in the opposite direction. I looked across the flat piece of moorland to another range of hills.

"There's a circular path, leading to the other side and up to the ridge," Sam explained. "It's not a difficult walk."

I wondered why I had been so nervous. His voice was gentle, as always, and he led the way.

WE stopped for lunch on a rocky ledge. Below us was the stony track we had followed and lower down the slopes, to our right, the green of forestry land. The bracken was already tinged brown, turning gold where the sun caught it. In the distance I could see a village . . . It was so beautiful.

All too soon it was time to move.

We were soon on the ridge and I zipped up my jacket against the breeze. The air was fresh, invigorating.

Sam located the path and slowly we made our way down. We were over the worst and standing on a grassy plateau when he turned to me.

"Any coffee left?"

I nodded and we sat down, emptying our flasks.

I used my haversack as a pillow and stretched out, closing my eyes, filled with inner contentment.

It was then I felt Sam move, felt his hands on mine. I opened my eyes to find his face was just above me.

"Lucy —" he said softly.

I jumped up, startled, sending my coffee cup rolling down the hill.

"No, Sam! You promised," I cried out in shock.

He shrugged into his haversack and picked mine up, helping me put it on.

Sweet Dreams

I OFTEN wake up dreaming,
Some strange, confusing dream,
Where people are familiar,
Yet are not what they seem;

Where getting lost is common,
My journey never ends,
When sad things leave me sobbing,
Unpleasant times with friends.

The happiest I remember,
Was dancing, oh, so free,
Exhilarated, joyful,
A gay, abandoned me.

If I could press a button,
Have dreams I choose instead,
I'd certainly be early
In going off to bed.

— Chrissy Greenslade.

Decision Time

IT'S time I had a clear-out,
I'm sure you've said this too,
When too much has been hoarded,
Old, useful, nearly new.

That faded pair of trousers,
Ice-skates I loved so much,
Wallpaper rolls, old lampshades,
Curtains, carpets and such.

It really isn't rubbish,
I might need it one day,
I sigh, for it's not easy,
To sort and give away.

So as a temporary measure,
I've put it in the shed,
With other "useful" items,
Which should be dumped instead.

At last I have a huge pile,
To give our charity shop,
Oh, look my tennis racket
Is lying on the top.

I hope no-one will see me
Hide it beneath the bed,
For I might wish I'd kept it,
In spite of what I've said.

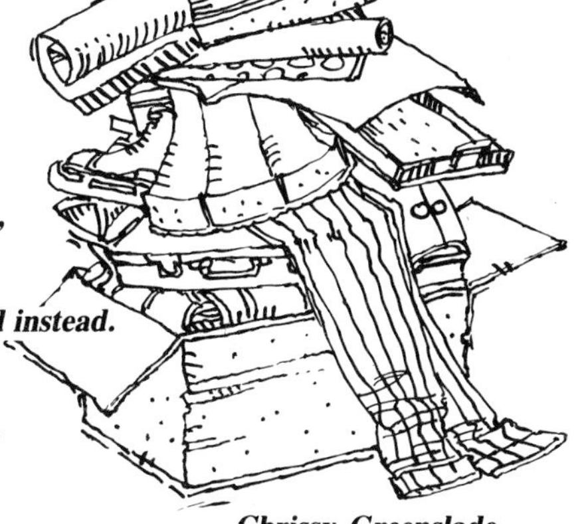

— *Chrissy Greenslade.*

"We'll go," he said gently.

We didn't speak until we were nearly back at our cars.

He put his hands on my shoulders, stopping me for a moment.

"You go on, Lucy. There's still a couple of hours of daylight left, so I'll walk a bit farther."

I looked up at him, gazing deep into his sad eyes.

"I'm sorry, love," he said awkwardly. "Only I thought, after all this time —"

I looked down and he took my hands.

"I told you once, you can't live in the past for ever. There comes a time when you have to open your heart, let out the bitterness, make way for new love, new beginnings."

He turned and walked away and I watched him go in the direction of the high ridges.

AS I drove away, his eyes haunted me. It was the first time we had parted without making arrangements for the following weekend and I felt disappointed.

Suddenly I didn't want to go home to a lonely meal in my flat. I was passing a small hotel so I stopped and went in.

I sat down in the lounge and ordered soup and a crusty hunk of french bread. Then I settled back with cheese, biscuits and coffee.

I thought about my day, about the quiet happiness I had felt when I was with Sam. We enjoyed our day because we were together, I suddenly realised.

I closed my eyes and let my thoughts drift back over the summer.

I thought about Nigel and was surprised when I felt no regrets. I realised it would never have worked out for us.

Sam, I thought, what have I done? It was time to begin again, but had I already thrown away my chance of happiness with Sam?

A small group of walkers were sitting down at a nearby table and I couldn't help hearing one speak.

"Thick, isn't it? Came down all at once."

I looked out of the window and saw the mist.

I quickly paid for my meal and hurried outside. I found myself in a whirl of grey fog.

Sam! He might still be on the hills, disorientated by the mist! I got into my car and started back to the carpark. If his car was gone then I would know he was safely on his way home, if not . . .

I was soon hopelessly lost. I must have missed the signpost in the thick fog. A break in the mist showed a huge crag at the side of the road and I knew I was on unfamiliar ground.

I pulled up, knowing it would be senseless to continue.

Ten minutes later I heard a car coming slowly along.

It was alongside me before the headlights even penetrated the fog.

"You lost?" a woman's voice asked.

"Yes, but I have to get back to the carpark . . ." I felt my voice rising and tried to keep calm.

A man leaned across the woman and spoke comfortingly.

"You'll not find your way anywhere tonight, love. There's a Youth Hostel a little bit farther on. I'm sure they'll find us somewhere for the night. Look, I'll go slowly, so just follow me." He smiled.

For the next ten minutes we crept along the winding lane, and then turned into a carpark.

There was a log fire in the hostel lounge with a few men huddled round it.

Roger, the warden, brought us huge mugs of tea, and my rescuers, Doris and Fred Norton, told me they had stayed here years before.

"I can't stay," I told them urgently. "You see, I have to find Sam —" I couldn't stop the tears which sprang into my eyes. "Sam stayed behind to do some more climbing —"

"Where did you leave him?" Roger asked.

"I can show you on my map. It's still in the car," I told him. "He may be caught in the mist —"

Roger was soon on the phone, but he looked grave as he came back.

"The police will try to locate Sam's car. Then we'll know if they have to call out the rescue teams." He laid a comforting hand on my shoulder.

"Hungry?" he asked.

I shook my head and Doris put an arm round me.

"Show us our dorm, Roger," she said. "I think Lucy needs to rest."

Doris lent me a nightgown and tucked me up as though I was a child.

I couldn't hide my tears. What if something had happened to Sam?

"It'll be all right, love," she assured me gently. "I know it's hard, not knowing what's happening.

"Do you love him very much?"

I stared at her.

Love him? I suddenly realised I did. How could I have been so blind?

"Oh, yes," I told her. "I love him very much."

I didn't expect to sleep, but finally exhaustion overcame me.

WHEN I woke I got up and hurried to the window. It was barely light, but the fog had gone.

I hurriedly dressed and went through to the lounge.

Roger was also up early. He smiled as he handed me a mug of tea.

"Sam's car *was* still there. The rescue party went out last night."

I held my breath.

"They found him with a broken leg. He was taken to hospital immediately."

"Oh, thank God," I whispered, tears coursing down my cheeks. "I must see him."

Sam was sleeping when I arrived at the hospital and I sat by his bed for a long time before he opened his eyes.

"Lucy." His voice was just a whisper. "The mist came down and I slipped. I managed to wriggle into my survival bag, and just prayed I would be found."

"Hush," I whispered. "You can tell me later." I smiled gently.

"I'm sorry for what happened earlier," he told me quietly.

I bent and kissed him gently on the lips.

"I'm sorry, too. I've been so blind. I know I'd built a barrier round myself. It was so stupid."

"You mean —" A tender smile touched his lips.

"You told me the time would come when I had to open my heart." I was smiling. "It came, my darling, last night when I realised how meaningless everything would be if . . ."

I felt his hand cover mine.

"And is there a place there now for me?" he asked, his eyes shining.

I nodded, suddenly shy.

"Oh, Lucy . . " He raised a hand to touch my cheek gently then tried to sit up, but the cage over his legs checked him. He lay back on the pillows, grimacing with pain.

"What a time to tell me," he grumbled, "but just wait. In another week or two . . ."

"I can wait," I told him. "Just as long as it takes." □

Say Goodbye To The Past

"MUM! The boat's coming!"

Kirsteen came down from the step-ladder, and was dusting plaster from her hands, when Nell came tearing around the corner of the dry-stone dyke that surrounded the croft. Lagging behind, a wee boy pedalled a bike which still had its training wheels attached.

"Toby and me were watching for the ferry all the way from school," Nell began breathlessly, bursting into the cottage. "Daddy saw us from the deck and waved — "

She broke off, suddenly noticing all that had been done since she'd left for school that morning.

"It looks just like a dolls' house! Grandpa'll love it!"

"Isn't it ready *yet?*" Toby declared disconsolately from the doorway. "When *will — ?*"

"When it's done!" Kirsteen laughed. Toby had been asking the same question every day since she and Malcolm began converting the stone byre two months before.

"Oh." He gave a long-suffering sigh and turned away. "I'll wait at the gate for Daddy."

"It'll be nice when Grandpa's living here," Nell went on solemnly. "He always looks so lonely now Gran's not there. Even poor old Snowy's sad."

"I know . . ."

It was almost three months since her mother had died, and Kirsteen was growing more and more unhappy to think of her father living alone in Portbreck on the mainland. Colin Petrie was fit enough for his age, but suppose he took ill, or had a fall . . . ?

They might not be very far away in actual miles, but the stretch of water separating him from Durinnock made the distance much greater. Kirsteen knew she wouldn't have any real peace of mind until Dad was safely settled in the cottage.

"I'm not being like Toby." Nell began to help Kirsteen tidy up. "But when will the cottage be ready? In time for Grandpa's birthday?"

"Oh, yes! We *must* have it ready before then!"

But later when she and Malcolm were mixing another batch of plaster in the cottage, Kirsteen wasn't so sure.

"The cottage will be finished before Dad's birthday, won't it? It's only just over a week . . . ?"

"There's still a fair bit to do," Malcolm admitted, glancing around. "But don't worry — we'll manage."

She kissed his cheek.

"Mum wasn't one to make a fuss about things like anniversaries, but Dad's birthday was different. She always used to make a big family tea, with his favourite cake."

by JANET SHORE

"Ah, Phemie's famous iced cherry and ginger cake!" Malcolm smiled down at his wife.

"It was her own recipe, too. And she only ever baked it once a year . . ." Kirsteen's voice caught. "I can't bear the thought of Dad being alone in that house on his birthday!"

"He won't be," Malcolm reassured, giving her a quick hug.

DURING the following week, Kirsteen and Malcolm travelled across to Portbreck as frequently as possible. Colin not only had to pack what he was bringing with him, but had to clear the big family house. There were even some of Phemie's belongings still to be sorted.

She'd been a thrifty woman, loth to throw out anything that might have any use left in it. Kirsteen found it a heart-rending task.

Colin watched her as they worked together in the attic.

Phemie had had a difficult time when Kirsteen was born prematurely, and been told there couldn't be any more babies. Colin swallowed as he recalled that first, frightening year when the tiny baby clung to life . . .

Phemie had tended to be a shade over-protective of Kirsteen after that, always anxious to spare her life's hurt. Colin hadn't always thought it wise, but he'd never found the heart to argue.

And it had done no harm, Colin considered. Kirsteen had grown up to be a fine woman, just like her mother.

"I'm a lucky man," he told her gruffly. "I've got you and Malcolm and Nell and Toby. I couldn't have got through these past months without you."

"Oh, Dad! I'm so glad you're coming to live with us!" She put her arms about his bowed shoulders, blinking back sudden tears.

"The children just can't wait. They've already told their friends that their grandpa and his dog are going to live at the bottom of the garden!"

"Makes us sound like a pair of gnomes!" Colin laughed, rescuing a woolly sock from Snowy before moving on to the next tea-chest.

"I've not been to the cottage since the builders finished," he went on cheerfully. "I'm looking forward to seeing what you've been doing to it!"

"Nell and I put the curtains up yesterday." Kirsteen gave him a watery smile. "Nice, flowery, pink ones.

"We had an argument with Toby. He wanted you to have curtains with steam engines chugging across them. So we compromised. Flowery curtains and cushions with fat little trains on them!"

"When I was a boy, I wanted to be an engine driver!" Colin chuckled. "They'll suit me grand!"

Still smiling, he considered Kirsteen's pale face. All this sorting-out was upsetting her.

"I don't know about you, but I've had enough." He got to his feet. "How about some tea? I got some scones when I collected my pension."

"Sounds great, Dad!" Kirsteen responded with a smile. "You put the kettle on, and I'll just finish here — there's not much to do."

Kirsteen watched him slowly descend the steep attic stairs before turning back to the tea-chest. She pulled out a bundle of tattered wartime papers from when Mum was evacuated to the country, then a toffee tin filled with buttons and, finally, a square black handbag.

It was old and well worn, yet she couldn't remember her mother using it. Opening it, she found a small, blue, glass bottle of perfume. She unscrewed the cap . . . a whisper of scent remained in the empty bottle.

It was so sad to think of Mum . . .

Kirsteen shook herself sternly. This would never do!

Briskly she removed a powder puff and a neatly-pressed handkerchief from the bag. Then her fingertips felt something hard and oblong which had slipped down into the lining.

It was a small grey notebook. From the date on the cover, Phemie must have been in her mid-teens . . .

Kirsteen opened the first page, feeling like an intruder. Mum hadn't kept it as a diary exactly, but she'd jotted down her thoughts and feelings from the time she'd left school and gone to find work in a glove factory in Glasgow.

Kirsteen continued to turn the pages. Some of the entries were paragraphs long, others merely a sentence. Several pages had been torn out altogether.

Still reading, Kirsteen scrambled to her feet, intending to take the notebook downstairs to show her father.

Suddenly her heart seemed to stop beating. The words before her, written in her mother's own hand, just couldn't be true. Couldn't be!

KIRSTEEN'S knees buckled beneath her. She sank down on to the dusty floorboards, clutching the notebook with trembling hands.

"Tea's ready when you are, lassie!" Colin's cheerful voice came from the foot of the stairs.

She couldn't answer at first.

"Kirsteen?" His call came again, this time anxious. "Is everything all right?"

"Y-yes!" Her throat was dry, she could scarcely speak. "I'm coming!"

Pushing the notebook into the pocket of her jeans, Kirsteen started downstairs.

She stood in the doorway of the living-room. It didn't look like the room she'd known.

Carpets and lino were rolled up and propped against one wall; chairs and the table stacked by the other. Pictures, ornaments and the large, fan-shaped mirror from over the fireplace were wrapped in newspaper and packed in cardboard boxes.

Suddenly, nothing was as she'd known it!

She turned abruptly, almost bumping into Colin as he came from the kitchen with the tray of tea and scones.

"There's a jar of your mum's raspberry jam to — " He broke off in alarm when he saw Kirsteen's face.

"What's the matter?"

"I'm — I'm sorry, Dad — " The word sounded hollow and empty. "I can't stay. I'm going home — "

"All right. If that's what you want," Colin agreed gently, thinking it had all got too much for her. He shouldn't have left her alone with Phemie's things . . .

"I'll walk you to the pier — "

"No!"

She darted past him to the hall and tugged her jacket from the peg behind the front door.

"Don't . . . Please!"

She pulled open the door, and was gone.

Colin could not have caught up with Kirsteen if he'd tried. But he watched her with anguished eyes until she disappeared round the corner. Then he hurried to telephone Malcolm.

AS Malcolm took the short cut across the brae, he could see that the ferry had already berthed.

He and the children had been laying the carpet in the cottage when Toby, bored, went out into the garden and heard the phone ringing and ringing. Colin had been relieved to hear finally Malcolm's voice. He quickly explained what had happened.

Leaving the children with their nearest neighbour, Malcolm hurried to the pier. There were never many passengers to the island this early in the year, and those who had been aboard had already disembarked. There was no sigh of Kirsteen.

Malcolm took off at a run past the fishing boats at the quayside and along the shore road.

Hazy drizzle was sliding from the grey afternoon sky and it was some minutes before he finally spotted his wife. She was sitting hunched on the sea-wall, staring out across the water towards the mainland.

"Kirsteen! Are you all right?" He reached her breathlessly. "Your father phoned and — "

"He's not my father, Malcolm," she said flatly. "Colin Petrie isn't my father! I was five weeks old when Mum met him. Two, when they married."

Malcolm stared at her blankly for several seconds.

"Are you sure?" was all he could say.

She nodded miserably.

"My real father is someone called Ralph Menzies, from Lanark. He was older than Mum and just out of the Army. He'd gone to Glasgow looking for work, just like she had."

Kirsteen opened the notebook and thrust it into Malcolm's hands.

"It's all in here. Read it for yourself!"

HIDDEN VILLAGES OF SCOTLAND

CROVIE (Banffshire)

CROVIE, on the Banffshire coast, is so well tucked away, between the red cliffs of Gamrie bay and the shores of the Moray Firth, that one wonders how a fishing village ever came to be built here.

But the coastal villages up this way tend to be like that. At nearby Gardenstown, it's much the same — the houses rise tier upon tier from the sea's edge.

In its day Crovie, well sheltered by More Head and Crovie Head, meant home to quite a few families, and gave a safe beaching place for the small sailing-craft of that time. The modern fishing vessels and crews have long since migrated to ports such as Aberdeen, Buckie and Fraserburgh, which have more spacious anchorage and selling potential.

Nevertheless, Crovie has scored in one way. Being so isolated and difficult of access, it has hardly changed with the passage of time, and is now reckoned to be the best preserved of all the old-style fishing villages on this wonderful coast.

When I went down to Crovie, I found the village and its setting quite fascinating. Head on the hill, feet more or less in the sea!

The only snag is that once you're down there, you have to climb up again!

Malcolm took the book without a glance, shoving it into the pocket of his coat.

"You're wet through! Didn't you notice the rain coming on?" he asked, stripping off his waterproof and wrapping it around her trembling shoulders.

"Let's get home, love." He gathered her to him. "We can talk later."

And talk they did, until the wee small hours . . .

In spite of being exhausted, Kirsteen slept only fitfully that night. She felt shivery and headachy when she went downstairs next morning to light the kitchen fire.

When Malcolm came down, he crossed the kitchen to her at once.

"Are you OK?" he asked, although the dark shadows under Kirsteen's eyes told their own story.

"I don't know," she replied frankly. "I'm so hurt. Confused. Why didn't they tell me, Malcolm?"

"I don't know for sure," he said quietly. "But I think I can understand it.

"Last night, I kept remembering those nine years before Nell was born. Remember how we thought we'd never be able to have a family and were planning to adopt?

"I got to wondering how I would have told a child — who was mine in every way but one — something like that."

"But Mum . . . that was different," Kirsteen murmured wearily.

"Yes. So was life in the Fifties," Malcolm said intently. "Your mother had lost all her family in the war. She was alone, and still very young when she fell in love with this Ralph Menzies. How desperately she must have wanted to believe him when he said he loved her and wanted to marry her. Then he deserted her when she needed him most.

"Can you imagine what it must have been like when she found out that he already had a wife and young family back in Lanark?"

"It must have been awful for her, but it's not that I don't understand," Kirsteen insisted unhappily. "It's just . . . well, first I lost Mum. Now I've lost Dad, too. Or at least, I've lost — Oh, Malcolm, everything I believed in and trusted has crumbled . . ."

She broke off, turning hastily to put the breakfast plates on the table.

"I'm a grown woman, with children of my own." She glanced back at him, with a forlorn smile. "Yet suddenly I feel like an orphan!"

"You've had a shock," he said, taking the dishes from her hands and holding her tight for a minute. "Give yourself some time. You'll see that nothing's really changed."

"How can you say that?" she implored, searching his face. "I don't even know who I am any more!

"And what about my real father? This Ralph?"

"Just because a person has a child . . . well, that doesn't necessarily make him a father!" Malcolm interrupted.

She moved purposefully away.

"I can't pretend I didn't find that notebook, Malcolm. I have to tell Dad — Colin."

"I don't see what that will achieve," Malcolm replied in his quiet way. "Wouldn't it be better to let the past rest?"

Kirsteen shook her head.

"I've too many questions. With Mum gone, Colin's the only one who can answer them. He's expecting me this morning. I'll go and show him the notebook. I have to face up to the truth.

"Please try to understand," Kirsteen concluded despairingly. "What else can I do?"

THE ferry didn't leave until mid-morning, so after seeing Nell and Toby to school, Kirsteen took the long way home.

Wandering down on to the pebbly shore, she walked close to the surf-curled water's edge, willing the fresh salt air to clear her turbulent thoughts and her throbbing headache.

Alone with the surge of the tide and the skirl of the gulls, Kirsteen rehearsed what she would say to Colin.

But every time she thought she had found the right words, a memory or conversation or comment would come unbidden to her mind, and she'd have to start again.

By the time Kirsteen left the shore, she knew exactly what she would tell Colin Petrie. And her headache was almost gone.

Once home, she did some housework and did a batch of baking before going to catch the ferry.

Kirsteen had the row of seats on the after deck to herself. She took Phemie's notebook from her bag, reading it again from cover to cover.

As she reached the final page, the boat was putting in to Portbreck. Kirsteen went to the rail, and allowed the little notebook to tumble from her hands into the billowing, foamy waters of the ferry's wake.

Colin was waiting for her on the pier, standing alone with his roly-poly wee dog. He hurried forward as Kirsteen came down the gangway.

"You're feeling better, then?" he said as soon as he was near enough to see her face.

"I'm fine. I'm sorry about giving you a scare yesterday." She bent to ruffle Snowy's wiry head. "I shouldn't have rushed off like that."

"Oh, it makes no difference. Never mind!" he returned easily, as they started walking.

"Dad, I know you'd planned to move into the cottage tomorrow." Kirsteen stopped so she could meet his eyes steadily. "But won't you come home with me today?"

"Move in right now?" he echoed in pleased surprise. "What about my clothes and things?"

"Malcolm and I'll collect them tomorrow," she went on eagerly as they approached Colin's gate. "If you just fetch what you and Snowy will need, we could take the ferry straight back."

"We-ll — " Colin rubbed his chin, his eyes twinkling as he caught her enthusiasm. "Aye, why not!

"But what's the rush? Couldn't we get the next boat?" he inquired minutes later, fitting his key into the front door. "There's no fire, is there?"

"There might be — if we don't get back sharpish." Kirsteen's smile was filled with warmth and love as she slipped her arm through Colin's.

"It may not be your birthday yet, but I've left a very special cake baking in the oven . . ." □

SYLVIA finished her housework early, and had all the time in the world to do her shopping. She sighed, looking out of the kitchen window — the grey sky promised rain.

It would be so nice to get away somewhere sunny, she thought wistfully. She'd noticed an advertisement in the paper that morning for a romantic Greek holiday, and had read it longingly.

"Get away to sunshine, romantic ruins, exotic foods and relaxation," it urged enthusiastically.

Sylvia thought enviously that it was a far cry from the week's camping that she and Jack had planned for their holiday. Yet that was all they could afford this year, after redecorating the house.

A touch of colour

I shouldn't complain, she thought as she collected her shopping list nd bag. She and Jack had a good marriage, the children were both ong settled . . . but there seemed to be something missing from her fe.

What I need is a new interest, she realised.

The postman came and Sylvia quickly sorted the mail.

Bills, of course, circulars and a bright postcard from a friend on oliday in the Caribbean. Sylvia thought sometimes that having a ealthy friend could be very frustrating!

She opened the last envelope and out fell a cheque — a refund

by ELIZABETH HILLMAN

from her gas account. She smiled as she slipped it into her bag, and determined to squander it on something non-essential.

Sylvia cashed the cheque in town, did her regular shopping, then wondered what to do with the extra money.

The sky had brightened, and she wandered slowly down some unfamiliar side streets, hoping for inspiration to strike.

She followed the delicious smell of baking to a small café and treated herself to strong, fragrant coffee and a hot sausage roll.

The waitress had an accent — French, Sylvia thought. She tried to imagine she was sitting in a French café in a small town . . .

She thought enviously of her friend on that sunny Caribbean island. It would be so nice to have a holiday abroad.

Sylvia wondered how she could brighten up her life, staring absently at the opposite wall. Should she go to exercise classes? What about an arts and crafts course . . . ?

She realised that she had been staring at a large olive oil tin on a shelf, the label brilliant scarlet and gold.

Sylvia studied it admiringly. In the centre was pictured a group of gaily-dressed peasants dancing under olive trees. Around the picture were bright coins or medals.

Sylvia decided she must have a colourful tin to cheer up her kitchen.

"WOULD you like more coffee?" the waitress asked on her way past Sylvia's table.

"Yes, please." Sylvia nodded. "And could you tell me where you get your olive oil from?" She pointed at the tin.

"I can find out." The waitress smiled before disappearing into the kitchen.

She came back in a minute with the coffee-pot, followed by a large chef.

Sylvia felt her cheeks redden as he sat down at her table.

"You were asking about our olive oil? It comes from a Greek store — the Mykonos Grocery. It's not far away." He went on to give her directions. "This oil is the finest in the world, and the shop also sells the best feta cheese."

As Sylvia finished her coffee, she wondered what on earth feta cheese was! She suddenly decided to find out.

She set out for the Greek shop, her step light. It wasn't often she experimented with recipes and she'd never tried foreign cooking. She felt a stirring of interest at the thought of discovering something new.

When she arrived at the Mykonos Grocery, Sylvia couldn't help feeling disappointed. The front window was small, and the interior looked rather dark. She looked in at the display and saw a pyramid of olive oil tins, some bottles of wine, draped with rather faded plastic grapevines.

She peered beyond the display to the shop. It seemed to be empty. She took a deep breath, opened the door, and stepped inside.

The store, though narrow, was long, and filled with a multitude of objects on the shelves, the floor, and hanging from the ceiling. She savoured the smells of unfamiliar foods and found herself lifted by the music which was playing in the background.

She wandered around the shelves, bewildered by the cans and jars with bright, indecipherable labels.

She passed odd coffee-pots, pottery dishes with painted scenes, tall wine bottles, tins, boxes, books, magazines, bunches of dried and fresh herbs, heaps of unfamiliar fruits and vegetables, records, even jewellery . . .

There seemed to be everything to make a Greek exile feel less far from home.

SYLVIA picked up a basket and began to choose a few things. She found a small tin of oil with the now-familiar label, a pair of oil and vinegar bottles in brightly-painted pottery, a small tablecloth and four napkins embroidered with dancing peasants, a record of Greek music, and a jar of stuffed olives.

For a moment, Sylvia wondered uneasily if Jack would appreciate the new cuisine — if she was able to tackle it successfully, of course!

At last she approached the counter where the meats, cheeses and pastries were displayed. The man there was like a statue of a middle-aged Greek god.

"May I help you?" he asked politely.

"Do you have some — er, feta cheese?" Sylvia asked rather uncertainly and shyly.

"Certainly. How much do you need?" He looked at her inquiringly, courteously, and Sylvia suddenly felt that any kind of pretence or affectation would be ridiculous with this man.

"I don't really know. May I try it? I've never had anything Greek before," she confessed. "I was in Helen's Café this morning and saw that olive oil label." She pointed to the tin in her basket. "And I asked where to buy it — and here I am. I've decided to experiment with a Greek meal."

He smiled.

"Well, of course you may try the cheese." He sliced her off a piece. "And may I make a few suggestions for your meal?"

Sylvia nodded, savouring the tangy cheese.

"This is spanakopeta," he said, cutting several slices of a strange pastry. "Pastry as thin as tissue paper, layered with spinach, cheese, eggs, onions, herbs and cream. Here is baklava, made with the same pastry, but filled with nuts, honey and lemon — the original ambrosia of the gods.

"Take some feta cheese for a salad with olives, tomatoes and lettuce. And may I recommend these ready-stuffed vine leaves for the main course? They're filled with tasty lamb, made by my wife, who is the best cook outside Greece — except for my brother, the chef at the French café! And, if you'd like wine . . . ?"

"Oh, yes." She smiled.

He also included a small book of traditional recipes and, as he was adding up the bill, a group of ladies came into the store. He hailed them and explained Sylvia was experimenting with Greek food.

They were instantly interested and added their own suggestions.

"Our church just down the road is having a big festival soon," one of them said. "There you'll see all kinds of foods. There will be music, dancing, arts and crafts as well. Please come! We will look out for you and take you round."

Normally, Sylvia would have felt embarrassed by so much attention, but she felt comfortable with their friendly interest. She found herself looking forward to the festival.

Someone suggested that she should have a poster to put up in her dining-room, and the shopkeeper soon produced a bright Greek scene.

Finally her purchases were packed up and she left, followed by good wishes from everyone there.

To her amazement, she found that she had been in the shop for over an hour — time had just flown.

It had been much nicer than the rather impersonal supermarket she usually went to.

Maybe I should do that more often, she thought as she set off for home. I've seen posters for international cooking classes. And I can borrow cookery-books from the library — and records of music from all over the world.

She felt a surge of anticipation at the thought.

THAT evening, Jack arrived home to find the house filled with exciting, unfamiliar aromas.

He went to the dining-room and stopped in surprise.

"That's cheerful," he remarked.

The new cloth and napkins with the oil and vinegar bottles made a bright splash, and the colourful poster of a boy and his herd of goats was pinned to the wall. In the background, the new record was playing.

Sylvia tried to feel confident as she served the Greek salad, hoping desperately that Jack wouldn't put a damper on her new interest.

He approved of the salad. The vine leaves and the spinach and cheese squares soon vanished, and leisurely they finished the wine with the baklava.

Finally, Jack sat back with a sigh.

"That was a real change," he remarked.

"Did you like it?" Sylvia asked anxiously. "I felt that my cooking was in a rut, and I decided to experiment. We can't afford to go abroad much, but we can bring other countries here."

"Sounds like a good idea," Jack said comfortably. "You can make a meal like that any time you want to."

Happily, Sylvia cleared the dishes, and while she washed them and Jack dried, she told him about her little adventure.

On the worktop, the oil tin label gleamed brightly, and she smiled. □

Sadie — Our Saviour!

SAYING goodbye to Meg was the hardest thing I've ever done. She'd been part of my life for so long, always there when I needed her.

Throughout the last fifteen years, she'd been my closest friend, sharing my joy and sadness.

She'd seen me marry and divorce, have two children, lose my mother and nurse my father through a long illness. So much in one lifetime.

We buried her in her favourite corner of the garden, beneath the flowering cherry tree. Matthew made a little cross out of wood and Laura carefully printed her name in red crayon.

Friends are always full of good advice at times like that. Get another dog is one of the favourites — but you can't replace a friend like that.

by TERESA ASHBY

My father had been left almost helpless after a stroke. I'd nursed him back to health, but I was beginning to feel that we'd taken a step backwards. Even if I were to consider a puppy, I couldn't have coped.

A month after Meg's passing, I took a tray into the garden for Dad. He liked to sit on the bench in the sunshine.

"Tea and biscuits, Dad," I said cheerfully.

He turned away, startled, but not before I'd seen the tear on his cheek.

"What a lovely day," I burbled, giving him time to compose himself.

"Yes, Jill," he said at last. "It's beautiful."

"Try to eat something, Dad."

He sighed and looked up at the sky.

"The children will be home from school soon." I smiled. "Then you'll have a fight on your hands if you want a biscuit."

He chuckled softly and I had to swallow the lump which had risen in my throat. I often found myself reflecting on our misfortune, yet what had I really to complain about? My children were healthy, happy and bright, and my father had practically come back from the dead.

"I love you, Dad." I rested my hand on his shoulder. "Please, don't give up."

"I don't know what you mean." He shrugged.

"Yes, you do. You've fought every inch of the way. You were winning, too, but lately, it's as if you've just given up."

He heaved a sigh and picked up a biscuit, nibbling at it before grinning at me.

"Happy now?"

Dad's decline puzzled the doctor, too. He shook his head and rubbed at his chin.

"Maybe it's a virus. But there's nothing going round and he doesn't seem ill."

"You're a great help."

I smiled and he laughed.

"I'm sorry. There's nothing physically wrong with your father, apart from what's left over from the stroke. And mentally, well, I really don't think there's anything to worry about there.

"Honestly, Jill, I'm puzzled. I've taken some blood, but I really don't expect anything to show up."

"He's missing Meg. The dog. She only ever left his side to come for walks — or to eat! Perhaps I should spend more time with him . . ." I mused.

"Then it'll be you I'll be calling on! No, Jill, you do as much as you can for him — more than many. If it wasn't for you, I don't think he'd have pulled through at all. Had you thought of another dog?"

"I couldn't cope with a puppy."

"Who said anything about a puppy?"

THE doctor was right. Dad's blood tests came back clear, and further tests showed nothing wrong. He should have been continuing to get better — but he wasn't.

It came as quite a shock when I realised half a year had passed since Meg died. Six whole months and I'd hardly had time to miss her. Oh, when I was watching a film on TV, I'd absent-mindedly reached out to touch her head . . . but . . .

Then it would hit me, all the sorrow and sadness. The truth was, I hadn't had time to grieve for her properly.

With my part-time job and looking after Dad, not to mention two boisterous youngsters, I hardly had a minute to call my own.

And Dad had been on my mind a lot lately. In fact, I hardly thought about anything else.

I tried all kinds of new meals to tempt his failing appetite. I even persuaded him to come for a drive in the car, but as soon as we got home, he'd sink back into apathy and I'd think, I'm losing him again.

What made it so much harder to bear was the fact that I remembered him so well as a young man. He'd been so full of energy and life, carrying me on his shoulders, chasing me around the park and catching me up in his arms.

He'd set off for a walk and always, always, I'd run out of the house behind him.

"Can I come, Dad?"

It was a kind of ritual. He'd hold out his arms and I'd run to him to be swept off my feet and twirled round.

He'd had such a zest for life, I sometimes wondered if some sixth sense told him that his active life would be cruelly shortened. He'd lived every minute to the full and it broke my heart to see him now, sitting out in the garden, a blanket over his knees, gazing miserably into space.

When he first came to live with us after the stroke, he'd been bed-ridden. I smiled as I remembered how Meg had finally got him up.

Dear Meg. She'd brought in a stick from the garden and trotted straight upstairs with it!

I followed her, wondering what on earth she was up to.

She deposited the stick on Dad's bed, then stepped back, wagging her tail like mad.

Dad lifted his head from the pillow.

"What's all this?"

She barked ever so softly and nudged the stick with her nose.

"For me?" Dad chuckled, reaching for it, but Meg was too quick and snatched the stick back.

It turned into a game. Every time Dad tried to touch her stick, she whipped it away, tail wagging constantly.

At last, she dropped it on the floor and it was all I could do not to rush forward when Dad carefully got out of bed to retrieve it. This time, Meg let him pick it up.

"Jill!" Dad shouted. "Jill!"

When I got to him he was laughing.

by John Taylor

The Farmer And His Wife

IT'S half-past nine on a November evening, and I've been sitting at my desk since seven o'clock.

Today has been a really cold day. This morning the wind was coming from Siberia, but later in the day I think it must have been from the North Pole. The rain froze and the yard was like a skating ring. I was glad to come in to Anne and a warm kitchen.

Anne has begged me for years now, but I've never got round to coping with her request till tonight.

EVERY year at this time I buy a new, large desk diary. I keep one religiously and write it up every night.

You would laugh at some of the things I put down before hitting the pillow. The odd things are usually about something to do with nature, i.e. "saw a heron in the burn," "found a curlew's nest with four eggs," and other items which are of importance to me.

I was in Cupar recently and bought a desk diary for next year. I spent an evening putting everyone's birthday on the right date in the diary. There are twenty-two of them — sons, daughters, grandchildren and other relatives. I really needn't bother, as Anne seems to remember them by heart.

"Would you help me down the stairs?" he asked. "I'd like to sit out in the garden. I can throw the stick for Meg."

"Of course, Dad." I'd been thrilled and from that moment on, he'd progressed in leaps and bounds.

How many times had I gone into the garden to find him asleep on the bench with Meg lying beside him? She wouldn't be sleeping, though. She'd taken on the role of guardian, ever watchful.

She had become Dad's constant companion. She'd been a friend to me, a playmate to the children, but she'd been so much more to Dad. She'd been with him all the time, keeping him company for the hours he had to spend alone.

No wonder he'd declined. He had time to sit and brood and think, and sadness had settled all around him.

THE following day, I settled Dad in the garden and left the children playing under his watchful eye.

I wondered briefly if he remembered when I was small, how he used to play with me. But my two had each other. Perhaps if there had just been one, he'd have made the effort.

"I won't be long," I promised. "You'll be all right, Dad? If you want anything, Matthew can get it for you."

"Thanks, love." Dad smiled. "Don't worry. I'll keep an eye on things."

Each year at the back of the diary we enter names and addresses of friends and relatives plus telephone numbers.

Anne's been at me for years to get a new address book and so save me the trouble of writing them out each year. Oh, we do have one, but I think it should be sent to some museum!

Anne bought an address book just after we were married. It's about three inches by five, has hard covers and an A-Z index.

The covers are now loose and the indexes for A and B are missing. I notice if you want to find the names for B it says — "see V"!

Well, I splashed out when buying the diary and bought a posh, black-backed address book.

Tonight I started to enter the addresses into this new creation. I haven't got far, but I've enjoyed going down fifty years of Memory Lane.

ANNE and I have only been abroad twice, consisting of a four-day trip to the bulb fields in Holland and a trip to Switzerland.

In the address book are the names and addresses of people of people on those two trips. We've never met them again, but you know how you promise to get in touch.

As I thumbed through the names, I came across one who sent a Christmas card to us up until about two years ago. It said against his name and address — near Skipton — cattle dealer.

Anne and I both like him and his wife, and I thought it would be nice to ask them to come to see us at the Riggin next spring.

I rang the telephone number against the address.

His wife answered.

"How nice to hear from you, John. How's Anne?" she asked.

Then I learned why we hadn't had a card from them — Albert had died.

"John, it's my fault, I should have written," she reassured me. "Your call has taken me back to that happy holiday we all had together. Thank you again. Give my love to Anne."

When I replaced the receiver, I gave up looking through the old address book and went to see Anne, who was making pies and other things for the boys for Christmas.

I felt very humble and glad to be alive as I watched her. There were so many names in that old address book to whom we wouldn't have to send Christmas cards.

Anne's the scribe in our household, but now I'm glad she made me not only buy a new address book, but start to fill it with names. It's brought back so many happy times.

I could never replace Meg, I knew that. But I could, perhaps, fill a void in Dad's life.

I'd never been to an animal home before and wasn't prepared for the shock. Not only dogs, but cats, a couple of ponies, three pygmy goats and several rabbits wanted new homes.

Two sisters ran the place. The younger, Babs, a warm, sympathetic woman, showed me round.

Hardly aware of what I was doing, I found myself pouring out my life story to her, ending up with why I was there. All the time, I was aware of a lonesome dog howling in the background. It sounded heartbroken.

"I'm sorry. I've gone on a bit, haven't I?" I said embarrassed.

She smiled and patted me on the shoulder.

"Glad you did," she said. "I think I know everything I need to know about you. We won't let an animal go to a home that isn't suitable — and we check up on them afterwards.

"This little dog here, for instance." She pointed to a small, friendly-looking terrier. "Can't abide children! Her elderly owner died — she'd have been ideal for your father. Not the kids, though."

"This one —" She indicated a happy Labrador. "Beautiful dog, lively, friendly — adores kids, but she's clumsy. She could knock your father over, then she'd be heartbroken."

"I thought it would be so easy," I whispered.

"We haven't finished yet." She laughed. "At the end of the day, you must decide, but . . . come with me."

She led me to the end of the row of pens. There, in the very end one, I saw Sadie sitting in the corner.

She wasn't sitting quietly. She was howling — a sad, heartbroken noise. She was the dog I'd been hearing since I arrived.

As soon as she saw us, she stopped and came over to me, staring at me through the wire. She seemed to be weighing me up.

When I poked my fingers through the bars, she shied away from them. I spoke softly to her, coaxing her to come to me. After what seemed an age, she came forward and licked my fingers.

"She's very gentle," I remarked, wondering how she would take to my noisy children. I'd already lost my heart to her in a way I never imagined possible!

"Her owners moved away," Babs said. "They put her in boarding kennels, saying they'd be back in a week — but they never returned. She won't give her trust easily, but if she's given enough love — well, who knows?"

"How cruel!" I gasped. "How could they?"

"Oh, it could have been a lot worse," Babs said. "She was never physically hurt, but her confidence has taken a terrible battering. She needs constant reassurance and can't bear to be alone. You heard for yourself."

"She'd never be alone," I said and Sadie wagged her tail as if she understood.

"And in our house, believe me, there's no shortage of love!"

WE'VE a huge garden — something else that takes up a great deal of my time and energy.

When I got home, Matthew and Laura were out of sight, playing in the wild patch at the very end.

I couldn't see them, but I could hear them. Dad, as always, was

CRICCIETH CASTLE, GWYNEDD

DOMINATING the popular resort of the same name on the Peninsula of Leyn, Criccieth Castle was built in the 13th century. Gruffydd, eldest son of Llywelyn the Great, and Llywelyn ap Gruffydd, Llywelyn's grandson, were imprisoned here for refusing to bow the knee to the English crown. After Llywelyn's death, Edward I captured the castle and used it as a focal point from which to put down Welsh rebels. Burnt by Owain Glyndwr in 1404, the castle was left undisturbed. Today it is in the care of the Department of the Environment.

CRICCIETH CASTLE, GWYNEDD : J CAMPBELL KERR

staring into space. He didn't even bother to read any more, but seemed to spend his whole life just watching time slip away.

"Dad . . ."

He turned and looked up at me, taking a moment or two to register that I wasn't alone.

He looked puzzled. Sadie, meanwhile, was listening to the sounds of the kids playing and her feathery ears had pricked up.

I looked at Dad's face. He stared at the dog and for an awful moment, I thought he was going to reject her. But Dad could never be cruel . . . he stretched out his hand and called to her.

"Come on, lass," he said softly. "I won't hurt you."

At last, she ventured up to him and sniffed at his blanket.

"What's her name?" Dad asked me.

"Sadie."

"Hello, Sadie."

She sat beside him, pressing against his legs while he stroked her head. He'd never tire of doing that, just as he'd never tired of petting Meg. When he stopped, just for a moment, Sadie shoved her nose under his arm persistently until he started to stroke her again.

"She needs a lot of love," I said and explained why.

Dad looked really angry for a moment. He could never stand any kind of cruelty, to animals, children or even other adults.

"Well," he said softly. "We'll just have to make it up to her. What made you get another dog?"

"Well, I . . ."

"No, it's all right." Dad patted my hand. "I know how you miss Meg. The children do, too. She'll be company for you and you'll be able to go for nice long walks again."

"I don't know if I'll have time to give her all the exercise she'll need." I bit my lip.

"I mean, she'll need a lot — Meg didn't want much, towards the end. But right now, it's love Sadie really needs."

"Well —" Dad sighed. "Perhaps I'll be able to take a turn with the walks. I don't intend to spend the rest of my life sitting here!"

It was the first time in months he'd given any thought to the future. It warmed my heart.

"I couldn't go far at first," he went on thoughtfully. "But if I gradually build up my strength . . ."

Matthew and Laura appeared then and Sadie brightened up. Children!

She ran to greet them as if they were long-lost friends. When I looked at Dad, he was laughing.

I thought of the people who had abandoned Sadie and wondered if they really knew just what they were missing. It was their loss, our gain. We were her family now and we'd never let her down. I think she knew that.

In fact, in a strange way, Sadie seemed to take over where Meg left off.

Dad didn't take her out of the garden, but he'd walk up and down with her, chatting all the time. She'd gaze up at him, entranced.

YESTERDAY marked the anniversary of Meg's death. A year has passed. A new era has begun.

The children planted some snowdrops beneath the cherry tree, determined that Meg should never be forgotten. We all shed a few tears.

Then the miracle I'd waited so long for happened. Dad walked slowly into the kitchen, measuring each step with care, and took Sadie's lead down from its hook.

Sadie barked merrily and turned round and round in circles until she almost fell over. She rarely barked, and I'd never heard her howl again, but she seemed to sense that this was a special occasion.

"Sit," Dad said.

She sat impatiently while he fastened the lead to her collar.

"Right." He straightened up. "Anyone coming for a walk?"

He'd only ever walked her round the garden before. Longer walks were left to me or the children. I held my breath.

"I'll come." Matthew grabbed for his coat.

"And me." Laura was already pushing her arms into the sleeves of her jacket.

I wanted to go with them — if only to keep an eye on Dad. It took every ounce of my strength of will to say I had something to do.

I did stand at the window and watch their slow progress down the road, Dad in the middle holding tight to Sadie's lead, a child on either side of him.

He got halfway down the road, then stopped. My heart stopped with him.

I held my breath, then realised he'd stopped because he was laughing!

My dad stood in the street, his head back, laughing so loud I could hear him. Tears ran freely down my face.

He was a long way from being well, but he was better than he was — and getting better every day. I could actually see him improving before my eyes.

I hurried to the hall, pulled my coat from the peg and ran outside.

I stopped at the gate. They had started walking down the road again.

"Dad!" I yelled.

They stopped and turned.

"Dad," I called again, feeling all of six years old. "Can I come?"

"The more the merrier," he called back and held out his arms, just like he used to when I was a little girl.

I ran to him, heart pounding, knowing that this time he wouldn't be able to lift me, a grown woman, and whirl me round.

But as he enfolded me in his arms and hugged me close, the feeling was every bit as good.

"Welcome back, Dad," I whispered, and he hugged me even tighter. □

Thanks For

INTRIGUED, I peered at the long white envelope nestling amongst the boring browns as I scooped up the post from the door mat. My name, neatly written in unfamiliar fountain pen, had a small question mark after the surname.

"Yes, still Debbie Mason," I said to it as I wandered through to the kitchen and plugged in the kettle. " 'Miss'. No handsome knight on a white charger has yet galloped into my single status!"

Pushing the missives from the gas board and the telephone company behind my crockery hen, I opened the letter.

The address from a town twenty miles away was unfamiliar. The contents were fascinating.

A photocopied grid showed some thirty desks — all named — with mine highlighted in bright pink. Oh, the memories! Second row, third from the back, with Janice Duncan on one side and Tony Harris on the other!

I read beyond the heading, "The Class of '78".

"In July it will be sixteen years since we were last together at Greenmere Primary. I am trying to get the whole class together for a reunion. If

The Memory

by
CHRISTINA
JONES

you are interested, please contact the undersigned as soon as possible."

The undersigned was "Carolyn Matthews — née Butcher". I smiled as I splashed water into my coffee mug. Of course, it would be. "Badger Butcher", perfect at absolutely everything. However, the prospect of seeing all my playground friends again was so thrilling, that I was determined to ring Carolyn as soon as I got to work and confirm my attendance.

Matthews . . . I pondered as I pulled my hair back from my face, tying it in the nape of my neck with a scarf. Who would have been brave enough to marry the daunting Carolyn? Was Janice still a flame-haired flirt? And Tony Harris? Had he really achieved his dual ambitions to become a spaceman *and* England's goalkeeper?

I was still smiling as I negotiated my Mini out of the garage block. Which ones would I recognise and, more to the point, how many would recognise *me*?

I SWITCHED on the lights in the shop's darker recesses, loving as always the smell of books and lavender and polish. Mr Jessop hadn't arrived so I piled the post on his desk and unlocked the doors.

As the early summer sunlight dappled the rich wooden floor, I wondered just how many of us had achieved what we'd dreamed of in that last year at Greenmere . . .

An inveterate bookworm, I was determined to become a best-selling novelist. Working in Jessop's bookshop was the nearest I'd got but, even so, I was blissfully happy. And happiness, as Mr Jessop kept reminding me, was the greatest blessing of all.

I dialled the number, wondering for a moment if Carolyn would be at work, thinking maybe it would be better to wait until the evening . . . After two rings the phone was answered.

"Carolyn?" I ventured. "It's Debbie. Debbie Mason . . ."

Her cry of delight was a complete surprise. Funny, but I couldn't think of Carolyn as anything other than eleven years old, slightly pompous, with her fair hair in long plaits, and her face set in stern disapproval.

"Debbie! Brilliant! You'll come, of course? July sixteenth, seven-thirty. I've booked the hall at Greenmere! Fancy us all being back there again! Oh, I'm so glad the letter reached you. I didn't know if you'd left the area — so many have. I've had to turn detective! Still, I've run nearly everyone to ground now — and they're almost *all* coming . . ."

I held the receiver a little way from my ear, slightly bemused. Was this garrulous girl really the ice-cool Carolyn? I suddenly felt a sense of foreboding. Had we all changed so much? Maybe going back wasn't such a good idea.

"Maura is in Australia and Alan is in America," Carolyn continued, "but them apart I think we should all be together. Won't it be fun?"

"Er . . . yes." I tried to sound convincing. "I've kept in touch with one or two people who've remained local, but, yes, it'll be great to see everyone again."

I put the phone down, deep in thought.

"Penny for them, Debbie!" Mr Jessop said, appearing at the door.

I started guiltily but, because he was such an understanding man, I explained about the reunion — and my doubts.

He listened quietly and then gave me a fatherly pat on the shoulder.

"Of course you'll all have changed, Debbie. That's what the reunion is about. You'll all cherish your memories, but it will be so interesting to see how your schoolfriends have developed. Whether all the hopes and dreams have been achieved, or changed slightly over time, or died altogether."

I sighed.

"I know. I suppose it's just that those days were so special. I mean, Carolyn has changed so much . . ."

"I expect you have, too." Mr Jessop said gently. "I mean, you'd look a bit silly in ankle socks playing hopscotch at your age, wouldn't you?"

I caught his eye and laughed. I was so lucky to have a boss like Mr Jessop.

"You go along to your reunion and enjoy every minute of it. Relive the past by all means, but remember that the present and the future are equally important. Now, shall we do some work . . .?"

IT seemed strange parking my Mini in the teachers' carpark at Greenmere. I felt a bubble of excitement as I climbed the worn stone steps, and I was suddenly swamped by memories of playing five stones on these same steps, scrambling down them on PE days clutching my rounders' bat . . . It really did seem only weeks ago!

The hall was ablaze with lights, a Gershwin tape tinkling merrily in the background. Taking a deep breath, I stepped inside. For a second I thought I'd come to the wrong place. I knew no-one! Then I saw Jenny and Tricia, two girls who'd remained in the area, and knew this was it. The Class of '78.

"Debbie?" The voice was slightly unsure. "Debbie Mason? Goodness — you've changed!"

"Carolyn?" I stared in amazement. I recognised the voice — but was this motherly figure really the overpowering Badger Butcher of my childhood?

"Come and meet everyone . . ." she gushed, pushing a glass into my hand. "Oh, it's non-alcoholic punch. I thought it was best, as so many people were driving. What are you doing these days? You're so glamorous — and you used to be such a mousy little thing!"

Mousy? Me? Quiet, yes. Shy, a little. But *mousy*?

"Actually, I'm working as . . ."

But Carolyn wasn't listening. Grabbing my arm, she led me

towards a throng of people all clustered round a trestle table of food, still talking.

"And you're not married? Still playing the field, are you? I married Vincent when I was eighteen. We've got three children now, and . . ."

"Vincent? Not Vinnnie Matthews?" I couldn't disguise my surprise. "Really?"

"Really," Carolyn said, her face wreathed with happiness. "I always had a crush on him. I was so lucky to get him . . . Ah, here we are . . ."

Surprise upon surprise! Vinnie Matthews had been the worst tearaway in the school. He wasn't a bully, but Vinnie was the ringleader in every childish misdemeanour — the one who never wore uniform, never bothered to do homework and always seemed to be laughing in the face of authority.

"Vincent teaches at St Mark's in Wallingford now." Carolyn was beaming. "I'm a wife and mother. I've got everything I've ever wanted."

Vinnie Matthews — a teacher! Carolyn a contented housewife! What other shocks were in store?

Carolyn had left me on the edge of the group, moving away to thread her arm through Vincent's. I grinned to myself. He still had a thatch of untidy black hair and a gleam of mischief in his dark eyes. I had no doubt he was an excellent teacher.

"Debbie! You're still as pretty as ever! Remember me?"

"Janice Duncan!"

Still flame-haired, Janice, my desk-mate, was almost bouncing up and down.

"Isn't this wonderful? Who have you met so far? What about Carolyn and Vinnie? I had no idea! Paul Harvey is a pilot now, and Jackie is a dentist. Jeff and Ellen are both in banking and . . ."

"Stop!" I grabbed her arm, laughing. "Don't make me feel any more inadequate. Aren't there any ordinary people amongst us?"

"Loads," Janice said, beaming. "Plenty of typists and shop assistants, a taxi driver, two builders and . . . Oh, I'm not Duncan any more . . ."

"I didn't think you would be. You were always the school heart-

LOCHINVER AND SUILVEN

THE fishing port of Lochinver lies in the far north-west of the Highland Region in Scotland. Dominated by the sugar-loaf shaped mountain of Suilven, this is a land of lochans and sparkling inlets flanked by sandy bays. The area is a paradise for fishermen, walkers, bird-watchers and botanists. Motorists, however, beware! The roads around here are not for the faint-hearted, especially the so-called "Mad Little Road Of Sutherland," the unclassified road connecting Lochinver with Achnahaird to the South.

LOCHINVER and SUILVEN, SUTHERLAND : J CAMPBELL KERR

breaker. So, who was the lucky man?"

"I met him at college." Janice blushed. "And I'm almost as soppy as Carolyn. What about you, then? No plans to marry?"

I shook my head.

"I'm perfectly happy the way I am. I'll know when the right man comes along . . ."

"You always were a hopeless romantic!" Janice squeezed my arm. "But so quiet . . ."

"Mousy, according to Carolyn."

"That's a bit strong." Janice looked at me appraisingly. "But, I agree, you were so pretty — and now . . . well, you're beautiful! You look years younger than me! *And* you're still single." She sighed. "Anyway — come and meet Paul and Ellen and grab some of this delicious food before it's all gone."

THE evening passed in a swirl of happiness. The years just dropped away, and the hall rocked with laughter as we recalled exploits and dreams. We all swapped addresses and telephone numbers and vowed to make it an annual event.

We all crowded out of the hall, leaving Carolyn glowing under the heaps of praise. For a moment I paused, letting the others stream ahead of me. I wanted to see the classroom again, just once more.

I tiptoed down the deserted corridors, amazed at how everything seemed to have shrunk. It still smelled the same — a cocktail of chalk dust and Plasticine and wet macs.

A light glowed from under Mr Rigby's door. I still thought of it as Mr Rigby's classroom even though he had long retired. I pushed open the door and was swept away by a tidal wave of nostalgia.

The three-abreast desks were still there. The blackboard, the maps, the paint jars! Of course there were more modern additions. A computer sat in one corner and a television set in another. There had only been one television set in my day; a huge monster in the assembly hall, and the computer merely a dream. I squeezed through the narrow gap between the desks until I found mine, second row, third from the back, and sat down.

"You haven't changed a bit!" The laughing voice echoed through the open doorway. "Debbie Mason — as lovely as ever!"

I jumped, feeling guilty. Was this tall, dark man with the smiling eyes the new Mr Rigby? Was I trespassing in his classroom? How did he know my name?

"I'm sorry . . ." I tried to stand up, feeling silly behind the cramped desk. "Is this your classroom?"

"It was." His voice was still full of laughter as he squashed between the desks towards me. "Sixteen years ago. I used to sit here."

To my amazement, he curled his long legs under the desk beside me.

"Tony?" I ventured.

He nodded.

"Late, as usual. I arrived just as the others were leaving! Janice told me where to find you . . ."

We looked at each other. Tony Harris had always been late for everything. I'd covered for him so many times. But then, all those years ago he had been a skinny, gawky dreamer. Not any more.

"You wanted to see me?" I gulped. "Me? Specifically?"

"Very specifically," Tony affirmed with a grin. "I've been kicking myself for sixteen years. And then tonight, when I have my opportunity — what do I do? Miss it!"

"It must be very time consuming," I tried to keep a straight face. "Being an astronaut and an international goalkeeper . . ."

"You remembered!" He turned to face me, as he had so many times in the past. This time, however, it was different. This time my knees went decidedly trembly! "Actually, I'm a gardener. I've got my own business — nothing grand, just me and my brother and a couple of weekend staff. Still, unless you've changed your name to Jilly Cooper you didn't become the world's greatest novelist, either . . ."

"No." I shook my head. "I work in a bookshop. But then Carolyn didn't become Prime Minister, Vinnie didn't become a villain, and Janice is very happily married. Maybe our childhood dreams were destined never to be fulfilled."

Very slowly, Tony lifted my left hand.

"No rings . . ."

"No rings," I said softly. "You?"

He held up his hand.

"Footloose and fancy-free and you're wrong about the dreams — I hope . . ."

I knew I was blushing, but I felt happy and at ease. There was no awkwardness between Tony and me. We'd known each other so well.

"I thought you were a disorganised dreamer," I said quietly. "I thought Carolyn was a prig and Vinnie a thug in the making. I always imagined Janice becoming some sort of notorious scarlet woman . . . and they thought I was mousy . . ."

Tony leaned closer. "That was sixteen years ago, Debbie. Sixteen years ago we only saw in black and white. Some things have changed — but not all. Sixteen years ago I thought you were the most beautiful girl in the world . . ."

"Do you remember that I kissed you here in this classroom after you saved me from yet another telling-off from Mr Rigby for being late? It was my first kiss," he reminisced, grinning.

"And mine . . ."

Tony slid his arm round my shoulders.

"I think we ought to have a re-run, don't you? Just for old times' sake . . .?" □

Printed and Published in Great Britain by D. C. Thomson & Co., Ltd., Dundee, Glasgow and London.

ISBN 0-85116-606-7
EAN 9-780851 166063